It was like drowning in a sea of sensuality.

BARONS OF THE OUTBACK

Rich, rugged…and ready to marry!

In the searing heat of Wangaree Valley,
where the rainbow colours of the birds and flowers
mix with the invigorating smell of the native eucalypts,
sheep barons Guy Radcliffe and Linc Mastermann
work hard to be at the very top of their game.
They are men of the earth, strong and powerful!
Their wealth and success mean Guy and Linc
are two of Australia's most eligible bachelors—
and now they're looking for brides!

Last month you read all about gorgeous Guy in:
WEDDING AT WANGAREE VALLEY

This month, read Linc's story in:
BRIDE AT BRIAR'S RIDGE

BRIDE AT
BRIAR'S RIDGE

BY
MARGARET WAY

MILLS & BOON®
Pure reading pleasure™

All the characters in this book have no existence outside the imagination of the author, and have no relation whatsoever to anyone bearing the same name or names. They are not even distantly inspired by any individual known or unknown to the author, and all the incidents are pure invention.

First published in Great Britain 2008
Harlequin Mills & Boon Limited,
Eton House, 18-24 Paradise Road, Richmond, Surrey TW9 1SR

© Margaret Way Pty., Ltd. 2008

ISBN: 978 0 263 86542 4

Set in Times Roman 13 on 14½ pt
02-1008-54263

Printed and bound in Spain
by Litografia Rosés, S.A., Barcelona

Margaret Way, a definite Leo, was born and raised in the subtropical River City of Brisbane, capital of the Sunshine State of Queensland. A Conservatorium-trained pianist, teacher, accompanist and vocal coach, she found her musical career came to an unexpected end when she took up writing, initially as a fun thing to do. She currently lives in a harbourside apartment at beautiful Raby Bay, a thirty-minute drive from the state capital, where she loves dining *al fresco* on her plant-filled balcony, overlooking a translucent green marina filled with all manner of pleasure craft from motor cruisers costing millions of dollars and big, graceful yachts with carved masts standing tall against the cloudless blue sky, to little bay runabouts. No one and nothing is in a mad rush, so she finds the laid-back village atmosphere very conducive to her writing. With well over 100 books to her credit, she still believes her best is yet to come.

Recent books by the same author:

WEDDING AT WANGAREE VALLEY*
CATTLE RANCHER, SECRET SON
PROMOTED: NANNY TO WIFE†
CATTLE RANCHER, CONVENIENT WIFE†

Barons of the Outback duet
†*Outback Marriages* duet

CHAPTER ONE

LINC checked out of his Sydney hotel after a late breakfast. An easy two-hour drive later he was cruising through the beautiful Hunter Valley, wedged snugly between the blue-hazed Brokenback Ranges, dominated by the native eucalypts. He had an idea the word eucalypt came from the Greek for 'covered'. Maybe it had something to do with the way the buds covered themselves, as though seeking shade. There were over six hundred species of eucalypt at the last count—Australia's gift to the world. It was the fine drops of eucalyptus oil in the atmosphere that gave off that marvellous purplish-blue haze. That was how the beautiful Blue Mountains some forty miles west of Sydney got their name.

To his mind, trees made the landscape. He loved them. He was first and last a man of the land. Sometimes he thought he and the land were one—pretty much the same primal feeling of the first

Australians, the aboriginals who had managed the land for 40,000 maybe 60,000 years. The white man, with his need for progress now almost out of control, was doing great harm to nature. The planet was screaming out for urgent change.

It was a brilliantly fine day, all blue and green and gold, and the unfolding landscape was like one of Hans Heysen's famous rural paintings that found their way on to calendars and postcards and the like. Miles of sun-drenched vineyards met his eyes, expanding to the horizon. Here and there he caught glimpses of glorious big rose bushes, bearing a profusion of flowers. He knew roses were grown in close proximity to the vines because their presence protected the vines from certain blights. Fruit and flower gave off a heady rich perfume and a riot of colour.

The Hunter was Australia's oldest wine-growing region, probably the most visited, and it produced wonderful wines. In fact the Hunter was a Mecca for those who relished gourmet food washed down with plum-coloured Shiraz, golden Chardonnay, citrusy Semillon or classic Cabernet with its blackberry flavour; a superb wine to complement every type of cuisine. He wasn't behind the door with the vino, having sunk a bottle or two in his time, but he still had a taste for a good cold beer.

Some parts of the landscape were reminding

him of Italy: the imported eucalypts, the golden
sun soaking into the fertile soil, the intoxicating
aromas of fruit and flowers, the open grassy
meadows filled with wild poppies, scarlet and
yellow, their papery petals bobbing in the breeze.
He was halfway to feeling good when for many
years of his life he had been swept by restlessness.
He had a dark side to him. Linc had come to
accept that. Now he took his time, savouring the
laid-back atmosphere of the valley. It held more
than a hint of the wild bush he loved. Every
country had its own landscape. The Outback was
Australia's, but the *real* Outback was farther on—
the Back O'Beyond.

He slotted in another CD and drove along with
it as he continued on to his destination. Wangaree
Valley. Wangaree was the legendary stronghold of
the mighty sheep barons and their descendants, in
particular his old friend, Guy Radcliffe. He and
Guy had been through school and university
together, and Guy had been a role model for him
in those days—a calm, steadying hand when he'd
really needed one. He remembered Dr Mallory,
the headmaster of their school, describing Guy as
'the perfect gentleman'. There was no getting
away from it. Guy *was* impressive. Linc, on the
other hand, was kind of wild—especially since he
and Chuck, his elder brother, had lost their mother

to breast cancer a few years into their boarding school stint.

It had torn his heart out. He still wasn't over the shattering blow. Never would be. He had been very close to his mother, even more so than Chuck. Their father had favoured Chuck. The moment he thought of his mother Linc's breath caught on a moan. In those last heartbreaking days she had become so wasted—parchment skin stretched tight over delicate bones, hardly a vestige of her beauty left to her. But even at the end she had been so incredibly loving, so selfless and *brave*, thinking only of them, her two boys, and his heart broke all over again. Suffering seemed to happen to the best people. His mother had been the one who'd held the family together. He was going to miss her until the end of his days.

Right now he had to make an effort to clamp down on his upsetting memories. No one seemed to realise it—he knew he projected the misleading super-confident image of a man right on top of things—but he was a pretty complicated guy, maybe even messed up. Only his mother had truly understood him. His father had been antagonistic even when Linc was a kid. He knew he had always asked too many questions—not trying to be the smart-ass his father had long since labelled him, he had actually wanted to *know*. He'd always had an enquiring mind. But his father hadn't seen it that way. To him, being questioned about anything was rank insubordination. Ah, well! He wasn't the first and he wouldn't be the last not to get on with his dad. But that was all over.

He was in the valley for the best of reasons. Guy had asked him to be one of the groomsmen at his wedding. Something he had kept from the family. He had wanted to tell Chuck, but Chuck could unwittingly be conned into admissions he would never have made on his own. The wedding was to be celebrated the coming Saturday. Guy was marrying a very special girl by the name of Alana Callaghan—'the most beautiful girl in the valley'—or so the legend went. Linc had been delighted to accept his friend's invitation. Besides it would give him the opportunity to view Briar's Ridge.

Alana and her brother, Kieran, had inherited the sheep farm from their late father. Guy had told him it was a good buy, and Guy was the man in the know. Guy also knew Linc was anxious to strike out on his own. Briar's Ridge just might work.

It would be a huge challenge, even so. He did have money of his own, plus a nice little nest egg he had inherited from his maternal grandad—God rest his gracious, loving soul. His father, Ben, as tight-fisted as they came, would have refused point-blank to lend him a stake. *Giving* was out of the question. The only thing his father would have given was a few tips to Scrooge. Except where Cheryl was concerned. Linc felt a burning in his chest at the thought of Cheryl, who could have answered to the name Jezebel. Cheryl was another pressing reason he had to get away from Gilgarra. Cheryl, the third Mrs Ben Mastermann, had taken no time at all to fix her predatory china-blue eyes on *him*, of all people. He had taken it as a tremendous insult—both to his father and him.

Now nowhere was safe. A woman hell-bent on pursuing a man who in no way wanted her wasn't a pretty sight. He might have earned himself a bit of a reputation with the ladies, but he considered himself an honourable man. Hell, he *was* an honourable man. His only option had been to approach his father and let him know of his ambition to strike out on his own. He wasn't about to tell him that day was at hand. Ben Mastermann had been known to wreck more than one property sale.

'Your place is right *here*!' his father, angry as a bull, had bellowed, veins like cords standing up in his neck. Ben Mastermann had been furious that his younger son was willing to abandon their family heritage, even though everyone in the district knew father and son were nearly always at loggerheads.

What his father *didn't* know, and Linc could

never tell him, was the problem he was having freezing out Cheryl. Their mother had only been dead two years before their father had taken Valerie Horden, a socialite divorcee and a long-time acquaintances to wife. That hadn't lasted, although Val hadn't been a bad sort—kind to him and Chuck in an off-hand sort of way. Not that they'd seen much of her, what with school and university. The marriage was over after six years, with a ritual exchange of insults, laying blame, and a hefty settlement for Valerie. Nothing like marriage to bring out the best and worst in people. Val, a dedicated sportswoman, had plunged in, but had soon found herself way out of her depth with the demanding and autocratic Ben Mastermann.

Then had come a long hiatus, but just when Linc and Chuck had thought they had good reason to believe their father had abandoned any search for another wife, without warning along came Cheryl—who had *seriously* been searching for a rich husband along with the meaning of life. That had been a little over two oppressive years ago, and even now Cheryl was only a few years older than Chuck, which put her in her early thirties. The two brothers had spotted her as a gold-digger on sight. Chuck had put on a tortured smile for his father's benefit—Chuck was such a good-natured guy, and he loathed confrontations—but Linc, who had adored his mother, had stood well back, realising there was going to be trouble. Big-time.

Their father still believed Cheryl had fallen as madly in love with him as he had with her. He even joshed her about her 'chasing him'. That was something Linc and Chuck definitely believed. Not that their dad wasn't a fine-looking man, but he was in his late fifties to Cheryl's thirty-two or three, and of course there was the tiny fact their dad was *loaded*. Some ladies appreciated that sort of thing. A rich older guy was infinitely better than a young guy who wasn't. There had even been talk of their having a baby. He'd wait for *that* to happen. The luscious Cheryl was obsessed with her figure, and he'd bet the farm Cheryl had no intention of getting pregnant. She would even convince his dad it was *his* fault without saying a word. Wasn't that the way with older guys who had so much to prove?

It was all kind of sad. Worse yet, *dangerous*. Linc wasn't a guy who frightened easily, but Cheryl had freaked him out when she had burst into his bedroom.

'You can't go, Linc!' She had thrown herself headlong at him, clutching him around the buttocks, kneading his behind through his tight jeans with her talons, her pretty face contorted

with what he'd been supposed to interpret as passion. *'You can't go and leave me. Just play it cool, okay, baby?'*

Play it cool, baby? He'd marvelled at her language, let alone her damned effrontery. And he hadn't been able to fault her nerve.

'You're married to my father, Cheryl. Or was that just for the money?'

She had looked at him with an injured little smile, indicating that was *so* unfair. *'I think you'll find I'm making him happy,'* she'd claimed, china-blue eyes smouldering not for his dad but him.

He couldn't disagree with what she had said about making his dad happy. His father was still at the honeymoon stage, and thought all his Christmases had come at once.

What else could a man do? He had pushed her aside, leaving her staring at him like some vamp in a 1940s Hollywood movie. Probably a calculated piece of play-acting. Either way, he hadn't been able to get out of his bedroom fast enough!

Not that woman trouble hadn't been a part of his life. He didn't go looking for trouble; it came to him. Married women had offered—cold-hearted, toffee-nosed ones too—but they had never been accepted. Married women were off-limits in his book. Not that he had even met one who had inspired an uncontrollable urge. It was

Cheryl who was at the uncontrollable urge stage. She had shelved all caution. It all went to show she didn't really know his father. Any man fool enough to lay hands on Cheryl would finish up a corpse, with his dad going to jail.

How good it was, then, to make his escape! He'd have made it long, before only the entire district knew he was the one who actually ran Gilgarra. He was the ideas man, the power behind the throne. Chuck was a fine sidekick, a good hard worker, but he wasn't an ideas man—as he freely acknowledged. Their father had all but retired to give his sole attention to Cheryl. He had left them with it. And not before time.

Wangaree Valley was distant enough from his family turf, in a region called New England in the north of the state, bordering Queensland. It encompassed the largest area of high land in the country. His mother's family, the Lincolns, had quite a history in the area. They had raised merino sheep and bred cattle for generations. The Mastermanns had come later, and they had prospered on the sheep's back. Now Linc was looking to raise a dynasty of his own.

He wanted kids. He really liked kids. Two boys and two girls. He didn't care what order they came in. Just let them be healthy. But he just hadn't run into the right woman yet—even if he'd never been lacking in girlfriends. There were those who claimed he had broken too many hearts, but that had never been his intention. Some girls just wanted to settle down the moment he met them. As for him, he realised at this stage of his life he *wanted* marriage, even as he feared some wild cat still prowled within him.

He glanced at the time on the dash. He had told Guy he would be arriving mid-afternoon, so he had plenty of time. Hunger pangs were starting up again. He would stop to eat somewhere—the Hunter abounded with fine restaurants. He knew Guy owned an award-winning restaurant on the Radcliffe Wine Estates, but what he was looking for was more like a good café; a fresh ham and salad roll would do, with a nice cup of coffee. A man needed a good café or restaurant run by Italians for that.

Australia had become almost a second Italy, which was okay by him. He had spent an entire year in Europe after he had left university, and been back many times since. Paris was Paris— unique—but he absolutely *loved* Italy. Italy appealed to the exuberant side of his nature. He was not a quiet man. Neither was he the hell- raiser he had once been. The hell-raising had really got a kick start with the death of his mother and the escalation of the abrasive relationship he had with his father. He had been overlong in kicking free, but then Gilgarra had needed him.

By one-thirty he was driving through Wangaree's town centre. It was a very pretty town, a showpiece for rural Australia. There were some well-preserved classic heritage buildings on wide, tree-lined streets, and from what he could see a few lovely little parks. He was almost at the end of the main thoroughfare, Radcliffe Drive, when he spotted a place called Aldo's. With a name like that it was sure to offer good Italian fare and a decent cup of coffee. He was very fussy about his coffee. His long stay in Rome had assured that. There was even a parking space just outside.

He drove up beside a shiny black SUV, then put the sports car into reverse, slotting it in as neat as a pin between the SUV and an old battered ute with the obligatory bull bar.

He was a long way from home and he couldn't feel happier.

A few moments later, he opened the handsome glass-panelled door to the bistro, inhaling the fragrant fug of good coffee, strong and fresh. There was a small curved foyer, and beyond that two steps leading down to a seating area. The area was barred by a young woman wielding a broom.

Casual, seeking nothing but a meal, he was now jolted into full alertness. In its way it was like being slammed up against a wall. He had grown cynical about a woman's beauty. But *this*! He had to drag in a breath as a force more powerful than he reached for him and held him in place.

The very air trembled!

The impact this young woman was having on him seemed to be dictating his every move, or lack thereof. He found it thrilling and disquieting at one and the same time. He knew he was staring— but then weren't beautiful women used to stares? This woman was his idea of physical perfection. Even his lungs were scrambling for a breath. Damned if it wasn't like a mystical experience. The thought amused and awed him.

Just as he was deciding how best to proceed, the Dream turned, enabling him to study her full-on.

Sensation rushed through him with the speed of light.

She didn't speak. Neither did he. He couldn't think of anything to say anyway. Neither of them made a move. Instead they looked across the span of brightness, staring at each other for what seemed an awfully long time. It was one of those moments that go on for ever, locking a man in. For all his reputation as a ladies' man, he had always held a pretty effective shield against woman magic. In no way was he guaranteed protection now. He didn't relish the thought. There was nothing wrong with being fascinated. Unless it reached the point where it upset his emotional balance. At the moment that was pretty precarious. He had sworn off women while he got his life on track. Yet here he was, caught like a moth in this creature's golden glow.

How had she arrived in this country town anyway? She looked more as if she had stepped out of a medieval painting. Her beautiful classical features were absolutely symmetrical. Wasn't that rare?

He canted a black brow, unaware his silvery green eyes held a mocking challenge. 'I hope you're not going to take that to me?'

If he was expecting an answering smile—a lightening of the fraught atmosphere—he got none. There was more than a touch of dismissiveness in her great dark eyes. It sent the silent message that she had met his like before.

'Don't worry, you're safe.' She spoke for the first time.

Daniela had, in fact, taken swift note of the stranger in town even before he entered the bistro. What she decided now was to disregard the dimpled smile, however sexy, and the languid, yet highly athletic set of the stranger's tall, rangy body. Six-footer-plus. Copper-skinned. Jet curls. Startling contrasting eyes.

Linc, for his part, had no difficulty registering that he had been summed up and found wanting. It didn't, however, temper the shock of sexual excitement. It was like a hot wire in the blood. He felt the sizzle, the palpable thrill that stroked the hairs on his nape, causing him to shiver. The thrill moved to his scalp. Hell, what a reaction—and with such speed and power! He liked pretty women, sure, but not one of them had ever affected him like this. He was even having difficulty not reaching out just to touch her.

She had only the faintest suggestion of an accent, but he had spotted it right off.

'Buon guiorno!' he said. His Italian was fairly fluent and he had kept it up. Italian-speaking communities were all over Australia. He held her gaze—indeed he couldn't look away—plotting how he could get her to smile. He was used to smiles. He began to picture her smile in his mind. 'Like me out of the way?' He gestured beyond, to the main room.

'If you would.' Daniela inclined her head. 'A customer accidentally knocked an ornament off the counter here.'

'I'm relieved to hear it. You look the type that throws things.'

'Me?' She eyed him, letting him know she was questioning his impertinence. He was probably well-used to women fawning on him. She wasn't about to join the ranks. Daniela was far less trusting of men than she had once been.

'Just a joke, ma'am. I see you don't like jokes,' he said, with a touch of self-derision.

'I have to *get* the joke first.' She put a little more distance between them. 'Unusual—a cowboy who drives a sports car?'

She spoke as though the vehicle might be a serious rite of passage for a guy like him. Cowboys obviously weren't high on her *wow* scale. 'I'm a sheep man, actually.'

'Really?'

He watched her press her beautifully cut lips together—fine, sensitive upper lip; full, sensuous lower lip—as though she feared she would burst out laughing. He was only surprised she didn't say, *How absurd!*

'Don't you like sheep men?' he challenged, hardly giving a thought to lunch now. Conversation was way better.

'I have to confess you struck me more as a cowboy.' She didn't mention her first impression had been that of a rock star. He had that same air of glamour, wearing his vibrant masculinity like a second skin. He would fit neatly into the Outback as well. Not as your average stockman. Dear me, no! Boss Man was more like it. Young as he was—and he couldn't yet be thirty—he had the *command* presence, the easy male authority. It was written all over him. Then there was the educated accent, the self-assurance he wore like a cloak, the pulsating energy. A bit of a dynamo, she thought; the kind that loved women but didn't really need them.

Linc thought he was holding up well under the judgmental waves that were coming full at him, but he was a little baffled by her attitude. He wasn't *that* bad, surely? He glanced down at himself wryly. He was wearing black designer jeans, an upmarket bush shirt, elastic-sided boots. Maybe his hair was too long. He never paid a lot of attention to his jet-black curly hair. It sort of looked after itself. And he hadn't missed the little flashes of antagonism either. This was a woman who could erupt! And, hell, she was the rarest of creatures: a woman who had taken an instant dislike to him. He liked that. It put him on his mettle.

If the trace of accent hadn't alerted him, her looks did: Northern Italian colouring, wonderful thick, swirling blond hair, side parted, curving in to just below her chin. The colour could have come out of a bottle but he didn't think so. There wasn't a dark root in sight. Her complexion was perfect—honeyed Mediterranean. The lovely features were classical, her aura passionate but restrained—as if she deliberately held herself in check. Her eyes were really beautiful beneath arched black brows—so dark the iris rivalled the pupil. She wasn't tall—maybe five-five in her high wedged heels—but her body was beautiful. Slender, but with shape.

The glory of women, he thought, slowly releasing his breath. 'You're beautiful!' he said, unconsciously investing it with real meaning. He hadn't meant to say it. It just came out as a simple statement of fact.

'Thank you,' Daniela answered him gravely.

She had been called beautiful many times in her life. Unfortunately beauty often came with a high price tag. It didn't always draw the right people. She had left London and a great job because she was being hounded by a man obsessively attracted to her and her looks. Sometimes, back in London, she had thought she would go mad thinking and worrying about it.

Linc had intuitively tuned in to her wavelength. How men's eyes must cling to her, he thought. Maybe that was a reason for her being so wary. And she *was*. No mistaking it. He could actually hear the defences going up. So what was a Renaissance beauty doing in a small country town wielding a broomstick? She obviously worked here. A cute little white apron was tied around a waist he thought he could span with his hands. Her dress, sleeveless with a short skirt—showing off great legs—was navy. A sort of uniform, he thought. She made it look chic. But the aura she gave off was downright patrician, even a touch forbidding, as befitting someone who had stepped out of a medieval masterpiece.

Maybe she owned the place? Maybe she owned a whole chain of bistros? Though she barely looked old enough to be a big success. Twenty-four? Twenty-five? As well as being beautiful, she looked highly intelligent. That had conveyed itself to him. A confident, competent young woman who knew how to keep mere mortals like him in his place.

His gaze came back irresistibly to centre on her face. 'Do you believe in love at first sight?' he asked, as though it was the easiest question in the world to answer.

'Doesn't everyone?' Daniela answered, calmly enough, transferring her midnight-dark gaze over his shoulder. 'Ah, here is my grandfather to take care of you.' She sounded relieved.

'You work for your grandfather?' It really wasn't like him to hit on a girl in this blatant fashion.

'In this case I am helping out.' Clearly she was making an effort to be polite. Far more the *principessa* than the waitress.

'So who am I talking to?' he persisted, watching a big, handsome grandfatherly figure with a crown of tight snow-white curls hurrying towards them.

'Daniela Adami,' she informed him, turning to pick up a dustpan filled with pieces of broken china.

'Carl Mastermann. My friends call me Linc. I've come to look over a valley property.'

'Ah, yes? Which one would that be, Mr Mastermann?' She spoke as if there were hundreds on the market.

Couldn't she risk a smile? It was important to him to see her smile. 'Briar's Ridge. It's owned by the Callaghans—brother and sister. Do you know them?'

'I have that pleasure.' She dipped her head formally, then made a move to walk by him, a determined action that managed to be enormously seductive at the same time.

He eased back, resisting the strong impulse to swing an arm around her and no doubt receive a painful electric shock for his trouble.

'Nice to have met you, Mr Mastermann.'

It sounded as if she didn't want to lay eyes on him again.

But that, Principessa, *isn't about to happen.*

CHAPTER TWO

WEDDINGS had a knack of working their magic on everyone. Linc had lost count of the number of weddings he had attended over the years, but the wedding of his old friend Guy, and his beautiful Alana, a luminous creature, with happiness shining out of her eyes, was turning out tops.

Wangaree was one of the nation's finest historic sheep stations, a splendid estate and one that fitted the courtly Guy right down to a tee. The wedding ceremony had been held in the station's private chapel—a marvellous place to hold it, Linc thought. Flower-decked for the great occasion, the old stone building was wonderfully appealing within its surrounding rose gardens, all coaxed into full bloom. The chapel had been built way back in the early days and was the perfect place for bride and groom to take their vows. In fact, his own throat had tightened during the moments when the bridal vows had been exchanged. The utter seriousness with which those vows had been exchanged he had found intensely moving.

The good thing was he felt he had absorbed a lot of the happiness that shone out of bride and groom. It had happened without his working at it. The best man was the bride's brother, Kieran, a terrific-looking guy; the chief bridesmaid was Guy's beautiful, elegantly refined sister, Alexandra. Guy had told him early on Alex and Kieran would soon be tying the knot themselves. He just hoped Kieran, whom he had only just met, would agree with his sister to sell Briar's Ridge to him.

He was sure Guy was going to put in a good word. Nevertheless he was feeling a bit nervous the deal might fall through. The property had been allowed to run down—he understood their late father had been ailing for some time before he died—but he knew it could be rescued and brought back to its former high standing. He couldn't say yet if he would stop at Briar's Ridge as he had big plans, but it would be an excellent start.

It was as they were coming out of the chapel to the joyous strains of the organ and the peal of the chapel bells that he saw *her*—with extraordinarily sharp focus.

She was looking exquisite. She stood out from the beautifully dressed crowd around her, as one would expect such a woman to do. Even the glorious multi-coloured lights that were now spilling through a stack of tall stained glass windows sought her out, suffusing her face, her glowing hair and her bare shoulders in radiance.

If his eyes had found her, her eyes had found him.

There was an expression that seemed to fit how he felt: being struck by a lightning bolt from heaven. He couldn't say if that was a good thing or not, but it sure as hell raised big questions. He didn't for a moment doubt it.

She looked away, as though she had seen his thoughts on his face, her thick blond page boy falling against her slanted cheekbones. If he were smitten, she was making sure he knew she wasn't. He had to change that. He didn't know if it was a wise decision or not. He didn't care. Despite all his plans he had been shot down in flames. Remarkable it should happen when he least wanted or expected it. He even had an idea he couldn't return to the man he was. Maybe the right woman might be able to save him, make all the pain go away?

A big *might*, was the cynical whisper in his head. She had said she knew the Callaghans. What she hadn't said was she had been invited to Alana Callaghan's wedding to his friend Guy Radcliffe. Now, why keep that a secret? Why act as though she was never likely to see him again? Perhaps she was as troubled in her way as he was in his?

He found he wanted those maybes resolved. It might shock and amaze him, but he wanted to know all there was to know about this woman. *All* of it. Even if he wasn't ready.

Outside in the brilliant sunshine—the sun was blazing out of a cloudless opal-blue sky—the rest of the guests, those not able to fit inside the chapel, were milling all over the manicured green lawn. It was as big a wedding as he had ever attended. There were quite a few children, all dressed up for the occasion—especially the little girls, in their pretty party frocks—laughing and bobbing in and out of the crowds, playing games as children had always done and always would. Massive cream-and-gold marquees had been erected in the extensive home grounds. In the shimmering heat they seemed to float above the emerald grass.

She had to be deliberately holding back, because he didn't see her again until they were all seated in the bridal marquee.

It didn't take him long to locate her. She was at a table for eight flanked by two men, one around forty-five, the other his age. Both were dancing attendance on her. The food was superb, as were the wines—lashings of both. He was seated between two cousins of the bride, Violette and Lilli. Both of them were extremely good-looking. Perhaps Violette had the edge, but even she couldn't hold a candle to her cousin Alana, Guy's beautiful bride. Linc yielded to their harmless flirtations, effortlessly doing his bit. This kind of thing he was long used to. Both sisters appeared to find him worthy of their attentions, but in reality his antennae was constantly twitching, almost completely given over to tracking *her*. By some magic means he was now a woman-watcher. And that was just plain dumb. He was a guy who liked to hold the whip hand.

The speeches were over—all of them excellent, hitting just the right note. Guy had very movingly opened his heart to his bride and all the guests were applauding, everyone was so touched. Looking down the bridal table, decked with what looked like thousands of exquisite white orchids flown in from Thailand, Linc could see a little tear run down Alana's cheek. He knew it for what it was—a tear of overwhelming happiness. Weddings were times of high emotion. What he hadn't expected was to get all emotional himself. He tried to stand back from that kind of thing. Much better to keep all the emotions locked up inside. Grief, abandonment... As a boy he had been so crazy he had even *blamed* his mother for dying, for going away and leaving him. And his highly confrontational relationship with his father he had to paste over. He couldn't bear to think about that poor silly creature Cheryl.

At last the formalities were over, and everyone was free to roam from table to table, meeting up with old friends, making new ones, joining in the dancing. A great five-piece group was playing. The guy on the sax was so good—the sound, the form, the phrasing—he would have been happy just to sit there, listening, champagne glass topped up regularly. Only Lilli caught hold of his shoulder, urging him to his feet. Someone with a professional-looking video camera started to film them. He guessed the Radcliffe-Callaghan wedding would make it into the glossy magazines. He might even make it himself. He didn't look too bad in his classy suit, with a pink rose with a bluish tint in his buttonhole to match Lilli's sexy satin gown. All four bridesmaids were wearing drop earrings of large Tahitian pearls with a fair-sized diamond above—a very generous gift from Guy.

'This is wonderful, isn't it?' Lilli gushed. 'Alana is my favourite cousin!'

He wondered about that.

After a while he felt as if he had danced with every girl inside the marquee except *her*. Every time he made a move towards her some other guy beat him to it, or one of the sisters clamoured for another dance. The elder one, Violette, was being rather forceful about it. Lilli had confided in him that Violette had been a long-time girlfriend of Guy's.

'He nearly married her, you know.'

He took that with another cup of salt. He had a feeling Guy was a one-woman man, and that woman was now his wife.

She must have moved outdoors.

Pleasant as it was, he was continually trapped by pretty girls, eyes shining, cheeks flushed. He couldn't be rude and turn them down. He needed to keep up his role as groomsman.

'Don't disappear on me,' Lilli begged, her bright blue eyes locking on his. 'I promised Mike here another dance.'

It was his moment to make a move. His decline into sheer neediness was so dramatic, it was mind-blowing. He actually *needed* to see the woman. He actually wanted to see her smile.

A lovely gentle breeze was blowing, carrying the mingled scents of Wangaree's spectacular gardens. A lot of other guests had drifted outside, most still hugging their champagne glasses.

Where was she? She couldn't have gone home. Guy and Alana hadn't left yet. Alana, as tradition demanded, hadn't yet thrown her bouquet. The honeymoon was to be spent in Europe, but the happy couple were staying overnight in a suite at one of Sydney's luxury hotels, before flying out to Paris via Dubai the next day.

Obviously she had decided to lose herself. It

didn't make him mad, but intrigued. He continued on his way, skirting the main paths bordered by banks of azaleas and rhododendrons, a positive sea of them, pink, white, ruby-red. He traversed a small ornamental bridge that spanned a glittering dark green lily pond before heading towards what looked like a secret garden. He was enormously impressed with the way Guy kept the place. The maintenance of the gardens alone was a huge achievement. Wangaree was a country estate in the grand manner. Even Gilgarra, though a top New England property, couldn't match it.

The fringing trees along the path kept the light a cool subdued green, even on this brilliant sunny day. His mother had kept a lovely garden, continuing to work in it even as she'd sickened. He remembered the delight she'd had in her roses. She'd adored the English roses in the walled garden. David Austin roses, he remembered, luxurious and wonderfully fragrant. Perfume had been a big priority with his mother. Her David Austin roses had done well for her. As a boy he had spent many hours helping her, doing what he had called the 'hard yakka', all the while drunk on perfume and contentment. He had an eye for beauty.

Cheryl, now, had no interest in gardens at all. Jewellery was her big thing. Chuck had shown a lot of spunk, demanding their father turn over to

him their mother's engagement ring—a large
emerald surrounded by diamonds. Their mother
had always said it should go to her firstborn's
bride. Whenever she'd said it she had always
caught hold of Linc's hand, as if she had something else lined up especially for him. He thought
it would have been her pearls, a gorgeous necklet
her parents had given her for her twenty-first
birthday. If he ever saw them around Cheryl's
neck he thought he might die.

Gradually the stone path was narrowing—he
supposed to enhance its secret quality. He had to
bend his head beneath a glorious shower of
blossoms from a free-standing iron arch that was
wreathed in a delicate violet-blue vine. It might
be easy passage for most people, but not those
topping six feet. He could be following entirely
the wrong path, but somehow he didn't think so.
He fancied the spell that had been put on him was
luring him on.

As he stepped inside the entrance to the walled
garden, flanked by two huge matching urns
spilling extravagant flowers, there she was: the
only other one to find that enchanted glade.

He had followed in her footsteps. He didn't
know whether to be troubled or amused by the fact
he was utterly besotted with some aspect of her.
Maybe when he got to know her it would pass.

There was that cynical voice again. She was seated on a garlanded swing that was suspended from a sturdy tree branch. Wasn't that exactly where one might expect such a beautiful creature to be, in her beribboned short dress? The dress was exactly the same colour as the flowers of the vine that grew so profusely up the swing's support chains, a porcelain pink.

He paused, looking towards her. 'You couldn't have found a more bewitching spot.'

'Hello,' she said simply. She didn't seem at all surprised to see him. 'You're right. How did you know where to find me?'

He gave a self-mocking smile. 'I just followed the magic petals. You *did* strew them for me, didn't you?'

'If that's how you want to interpret it.' Her glance held faint irony, as though she thought it wouldn't hurt him to be taken down a peg.

'It doesn't matter,' he said, moving over the daisy-flecked green turf towards her. 'I did find you.'

'You were looking.' It wasn't a question.

No point in denying it. He ran a hand through his shock of black hair, pushing back the unruly lock that had fallen forward onto his brow. 'I've been trying to get to your side for hours.'

She began to swing, very gently. 'How could you possibly fit me in between partners? You were never short of one.' The minute it was out of her mouth, Daniela regretted it. It sounded as if she had been keeping an eye on him. She hadn't been. Well, maybe she had directed a *few* glances.

'That thing actually works?' he asked, his gaze on the swing, wondering if it was safe. It looked more like a marvellous decorative element in the garden than functional.

'You can see it does.' She began to swing higher. 'The garlands are a lovely idea, don't you think? The flowers spring from these little planter boxes fixed to the base of the swing. See?' She slowed to point them out. 'It's the most amazing garden. I love it. I expect fairies with wonderful sparkling wings hold midnight parties here.'

He could feel the impact of her—her beauty and mystique—in every cell of his body. 'Do you suppose they ask mere mortals to join in? Why didn't you tell me you were coming to the wedding?'

She flew a little higher. 'It didn't seem to me we would meet again.'

'Oddly, I don't believe you.' A good thing she was a featherweight, but he was still getting anxious. He didn't want to see her fall.

Abruptly she slowed again. 'Perhaps you're too sure of yourself?' She knew she sounded touchy, prickly, but she couldn't seem to control it.

'And the idea upsets you? What sort of man do you like?' He moved, his hands reaching out for the flower-decked chains, testing them. They held very firm under pressure and he began to propel her forward.

'I'll recognise him if I ever find him!' she exclaimed, sounding a little breathless.

'Tell me. What's a young woman like you doing here all by yourself on a swing?'

'All by myself?' Briefly she met his eyes. 'I thought you were with me, pushing me?'

'Aren't I expected to in such a situation? Hold still for a moment,' he cautioned, as on a downward motion a thick green tendril sprang out from the vine and hooked into her hair.

Immediately her small high-arched feet in their pretty high-heeled gilded sandals anchored her to the ground.

He freed her. A small thing, but it hit him hard. She put up a hand to smooth her hair a mere second before he drew his away.

Skin on skin. He could have been wrong, but it seemed like an effort for *both* of them to pull away. Was he crazy? He wanted to pull her off that swing, pull her into his arms, make love to her there and then. Such was his physical turmoil.

Perhaps something of what he was feeling got through to her, because she gave him a look that came close to a plea. 'It's better if we return to the reception.'

'As you wish.' He inclined his head. 'Is there any particular reason you don't want to be alone with me, Daniela?'

His use of her name affected her. He had a good voice. A voice to listen to. Voices were important to her. She slid off the seat of the swing, then stood to face him. 'You flatter yourself, Mr Mastermann.'

'I think not,' he contradicted. 'And it's Linc. Or Carl, if you prefer.' His mother had been the only one to call him Carl. 'Lincoln was my mother's maiden name. It's something of a tradition within pastoral families to include the mother's maiden name among the baptismal names.'

She tilted her luminous head. 'I have heard of it, though I've never had the pleasure of mixing in such elevated circles. You say your friends call you Linc? I'll call you Carl.' She knew she was being perverse, but she felt a powerful warning to keep her feet very firmly on the ground. Linc Mastermann was a charmer, and a dangerous one. Not for a minute could she forget that. He wasn't an *easy* man, either. She had already taken soundings of his depths.

'So tell me about you?' he was asking as they moved out of the glade. 'All I know so far is you're

Daniela Adami. You're home from London—your grandfather told me—where you were *sous chef* in a famous three Michelin star restaurant. Why did you come home, given you had such a great career going for you? Or do you plan to go back some time soon?'

She took her time answering. 'I'm here to see my family. I'd been missing them so much. Italian families are like that. They crave togetherness. Besides, I haven't had a vacation in quite some time.'

He wondered briefly, cynically, if his family were missing *him*. Chuck would be, but Chuck had found himself a girlfriend—Louise Martin. He couldn't have been more pleased for them. Louise was a great girl. 'You were born in Italy?' he asked.

She shook her head. 'I'm first-generation Australian. Everyone in my family loves Australia. We feel at home here, but my parents and my grandfather like to make a trip home to Italy at least every couple of years to see relatives.'

Again he had to bend his head beneath flowery boughs, while she passed beneath them un-scathed. 'I spent a whole year in Italy after I finished university. Rome, mostly,' he told her.

'They do say all roads lead there.'

'*Ecco Roma!*' he exclaimed, falling back ef-fortlessly into Italian.

She paused to look up at him. He was so very

much taller she had to tilt her head back. 'Your accent is good.'

'I must have a good ear,' he said. 'At least that's what I was told. For someone born in Australia, you still retain a trace of your accent.'

'I know.' Just the merest flash of a smile. He all but missed it. 'We're bilingual as a family. Actually, I speak French as well. It's been a big help to me in my line of work.'

'As a chef?'

'Yes.'

'I'm surprised you don't speak fifteen languages.' He made an attempt to get a bigger smile from her. Longer. 'Sing, paint, play the piano, maybe even the harp? What you *don't* look like is you eat much of your own cooking!' he mocked gently. 'You're what? One hundred and two, one hundred and four pounds?' His downbent gaze lightly skimmed her petite figure.

He loved her dress, just a slip of a thing that left her golden arms and lovely legs bare. Low oval neck, short skirt—simplicity itself. Only what it was made of turned it into a work of art.

'Why are you looking at me like that?' she asked, turning her great dark eyes on him almost with censure.

'Actually, I was looking at your dress. What is it made of? Beribboned lace?'

She kept walking, twirling a perfumed pink blossom in her hand. 'If you must know it's embroidered crocheted cotton by a top designer.'

'Okay, I'm impressed.' He laughed in his throat.

'Thank you.' She coloured just a tiny bit. 'I bought it in London. It wasn't cheap.'

'Worth every penny, I'd say,' he said dryly. 'You should never take it off. So, how long is the vacation going to be?' How much time did he have? God, was he *mad*? This woman was drawing him deeper and deeper beneath her spell.

'I'm in no hurry to go back,' she said.

She couldn't tell him she feared to go back. She had told no one. Not even her family. Gerald Templeton, the only son of a very wealthy and influential upper-class family, a man about town in swinging London, had in a short period of time become obsessively attracted to her—to the extent he had turned into a stalker when she'd told him she no longer wanted to see him. It wasn't beyond him to follow her to Australia if he could track her down. All it took was a plane ticket.

He saw the shadow that crossed her face. 'Sounds like this vacation is more like an escape?' He was following a gut feeling. Chuck always did say he was good at interpreting vibes. Besides, one could learn crucial things through instinct and gut feelings.

She said nothing. She reached out to pick another flower, twirling it beneath her small straight nose. 'You told me you were interested in the Callaghan place—Briar's Ridge?' She changed the subject.

He nodded. 'Very much so. I have Alana's okay; now I have to get her brother's. I only met Kieran today, and we haven't had time to talk. I heard he's become a real someone in the art world, and I know Alex is involved. Guy and I went to the same school, where he was sort of like my mentor. Anyway, he kept me in check.'

'You were a bad boy?' She looked up into his undeniably handsome, charismatic face.

He gave a twisted smile, deepening those dimples. 'In some ways, yes.'

'I have observed your dark side,' she commented, pausing to admire a stone cupid. Someone had placed a mixed bouquet of flowers in the cupid's lap. A romantic touch.

'Now, how the heck did you manage to do that?' he asked wryly.

'A woman's instinct,' she said, turning to allow her eyes to roam his face.

'Maybe you would have made a good psychologist, had you followed that path.'

'Maybe I would. Do…do you have a girlfriend? Someone you care about?'

'Is this simple curiosity, Daniela?' His silvery green gaze, made even more startling against his darkly tanned skin, openly mocked her.

She walked on, picking up pace. 'All right, don't tell me.'

He caught her up easily. 'Like most guys, I've had plenty of girlfriends, but no one in particular. Tell me about the guy in London. The one you're on the run from.'

She felt a violent thrill of shock. 'I don't know what you're talking about.'

'It would explain why you're so wary.' He spoke tautly, angry at the very thought some guy might have been hassling her.

'You're way off the mark.' She wasn't going to tell him he had scored a bullseye.

'Am I? You're a beautiful woman. A lot of beautiful women feed on their own self-regard. At least that's been my experience. You're not like that. You don't see your beauty as something special, more a danger. Am I right?'

What else had he learned about her? 'Maybe I'm beautiful only by *your* set of criteria?' she suggested evasively.

'Nonsense,' he clipped off. 'You'd warrant a double take anywhere. Unfortunately it's in some men's nature to hunt beautiful women.'

She stood looking up at him, trying to hide her

emotions. 'Why are you speaking to me like this? You don't know anything about me.'

'You don't know anything about *me*,' he countered. 'Yet you said I have a dark side. I assure you, hunting beautiful women is not my style. So you can relax. I had a mother I adored. I would hate to throw a scare into any woman.'

She believed him. He would never do so deliberately. 'You said *had*?' She changed the subject again. 'Your mother is dead?'

'Breast cancer.' His tone, considering how he felt, was extraordinarily level—even matter-of-fact.

It didn't fool her. 'And after she died you didn't know how you were going to go on with life?' she suggested gently. 'You must have been a boy?'

There was definitely something between the two of them now. 'Are you deliberately turning the tables, Daniela? I was twelve, my brother Charles eighteen months older. Sad, sad times for both of us.'

She kept her eyes on him, fascinated and disturbed by his dark good looks and magnetic presence. 'And your father? Was he able to offer much love and support? He, too, must have been devastated.'

'Oh, he was!' He could hear the cutting cynicism in his own voice. 'He remarried barely two years later.'

'A younger woman?' She felt his world of anger, pain and bitter resentment.

'Young women *are* nectar to older men,' he said with a twisted smile, 'but my dad's second wife, Valerie, was in the same age group. She'd been a long-time acquaintance of both my parents. Cheryl, on the other hand, is around Chuck's age.'

'I see,' she said quietly. 'It sounds like Cheryl is the wrong kind of woman?' The raven loop of hair had fallen forward on his tanned forehead again. She saw it annoyed him, but she thought it very dashing.

'It sounds like your womanly instincts are far too acute,' he drawled. 'Are you going to dance with me?'

She shook her head and walked on. Guests were spread out across the magnificent grounds, all laughing and talking, thoroughly enjoying their beautiful surroundings and the magic of the day. 'No.'

'Isn't that a bit harsh?'

'Maybe,' she said calmly. 'But I have serious reservations about becoming too friendly with you, Carl Mastermann.'

That didn't surprise him. He had concerns himself. 'Well, at least you don't fool around. You get right to the point. Is it because I have a dark side?'

Now she did smile at him. The first real smile he had received. It was so beautiful it took his breath away. 'Because you also have a *light* side,' she said. 'Maybe it's even brilliant on occasions. You're a mixture of both.'

'And this makes it impossible for us to be friends?'

'Is that what this is? *Friendship* that is passing between us?' she asked with a gentle air of melancholy.

'Maybe not.' Both of them seemed caught in a whirlpool. 'But if I'm a mix, so are you.'

'No, no!' She shook her blond hair so the heavier side fell forward to hide her profile. 'I have always been a very happy person, much cared for by a loving family.'

'Only someone came along to change all that?'

It was a troubling challenge. He saw too much. 'Let's drop it, shall we?'

'Certainly,' he assented, 'as it clearly bothers you. Just one condition. You break your newly established set of rules and dance with me. It need only be one time.'

In an instant he knew she was going to consent.

CHAPTER THREE

THE day after the buying of Briar's Ridge was
settled—Kieran had been delighted by Linc's
offer, and because he had a substantial deposit
and the bank on side, it took no time at all—Linc
drove into town. Not a single night had he slept
properly since his friend's wedding. If he wasn't
lying awake thinking about Daniela, how they
had danced together, the way she had let him hold
her, she insinuated herself into his dreams. He
even felt her in his bed. He woke with her fragrance on his skin.

You're crazy, Mastermann! His inner voice said
in disgust. *Give up while you've got a chance.*

He was so far gone he was indifferent to the
voice. There could be nothing remarkable about
his calling in at the bistro, he reasoned. Say hello,
then ask her if she would like to see over the
property he had so very recently acquired. He
knew she was resisting him at one level, as if she

knew she *ought* to—wasn't he feeling something of the same thing?—but they seemed to share a powerful kinship. How was that so? In many ways she was a mystery to him, yet he had been seduced on sight. Drawn closer. He thought he recognised her soul. When they had danced together at Guy's wedding he'd felt as though she belonged to him. Even their bodies seemed to recognise one another.

That sort of thing didn't happen often. It had never happened to him, and he had held lots of pretty girls in his arms, made love to them, learned much. But he had never come close to a grand passion, the great enduring love lady novelists liked to write about. He remembered hearing his mother crying quietly during the nights his father was away from home. That had been when he was just a little kid, stealing along the hallway, checking on her but not wanting to intrude on her very private time. He couldn't have borne to humiliate her, but the sound still haunted him.

What had she been crying about? His old man's infidelities? The way he had turned from her when she'd first been diagnosed? Or how he never touched her after she had lost a breast and her glorious mane of hair? His dad had an irrational fear of sickness, but that didn't excuse his cruelty. Linc thanked God he had been around to console his mother. Even Chuck hadn't wanted to know how sick their mother was, though he'd been heartbroken and contrite afterwards.

Since leaving home, Linc had kept in regular touch with Chuck. Chuck sounded as if he was missing him like hell—especially in running the big sheep farm. But Chuck, good brother that he was, had been genuinely thrilled for him when he'd told him about Briar's Ridge.

'Man, I couldn't be more pleased for you. You always have to do things in your own way. And do them better than anyone else.'

'For the love of God don't tell Cheryl where I am.'

Chuck, who had eyes in his head that had been very uncomfortable with their stepmother's attraction to his younger brother, had assured him he wouldn't say a word.

'Dad still mad?'

'Filthy!' Chuck had crowed. 'Maybe he never told you—it would have killed him to do so—but he relied on you one hell of a lot. Come to that, so did I.'

'I'll keep in touch, Bro.'

At least Chuck would have his Louise. He wouldn't be a bit surprised if they didn't set a wedding date some time soon. And eventually Chuck would inherit half of Gilgarra; he would get the other half. His dad couldn't do anything about that. It had been Lincoln money, his mother's dowry, that had given their father his giant step-up. Never let that be forgotten. They were entitled. Linc wouldn't believe in Cheryl's providing their father with yet another heir until he held the baby in his own hands.

When he arrived at the bistro he found it crowded with happy customers. Aldo, a most genial man, caught sight of him and hurried towards him, beckoning. '*Buon giorno*, Linc. You want lunch? I can find you a table.' His dark eyes swiftly scanned the room for a spot to fit in a single table.

Linc smiled, looking around him. 'Everyone looks happy. Business is booming.'

'My darling Daniela must take the credit,' Aldo said, goodnaturedly leaning a hand on Linc's shoulder. 'She's running the kitchen. Word gets around. We're banked up Wednesday through Friday. We like her to relax at the weekend. She's a genius in the kitchen. She is teaching us all such a lot.'

'In that case, it's lunch.' He smiled. 'And I was hoping to speak to Daniela when she's not busy.'

'I don't see why not.' Aldo looked closely into Linc's eyes. 'You've bought the Callaghan farm?'

'All settled. I was hoping Daniela might like to take a look at the homestead. You, too, when it suits. It's good to have a woman's opinion on furnishings. Especially one with such style.'

Aldo blew a gentle breath. 'The man who wins my Daniela will be getting a goddess,' he said.

'Lovely thought!' Linc smiled back.

For the next hour Linc enjoyed food the gods might order. Aldo was right. His little Daniela was one hell of a chef. He didn't have to wonder why she had chosen that particular career. Her family had always been involved in restaurants, Aldo had told him. It had been a big upheaval coming to Australia, and they had arrived with little money, but in the end it had been well worth it.

Linc had found that eating and drinking was a national pastime in Italy, and that little bars, cafés and bistros were the mainstay of Italian life. He had loved the markets and all the wonderful fresh produce. Every city, every town, every village had at least one. He remembered how the women had appeared to spend a large part of their day—*every* day—going to the markets. Food and its preparation was a very serious business.

Daniela would have gravitated to a chef's career naturally. Not that what was on the menu here was solely Italian food. Definitely no pizzas. Linc started off with smoked eggplant with a marvellous crab sauce, followed by *abbacchio alla Romana,* which simply meant baby lamb, Roman-style. It melted in his mouth. He thought he couldn't fit in a dessert—he wasn't used to eating a big meal midday, or even stopping work a lot of the time—but a slice of the mascarpone sponge with a berry and rum sauce looked irresistible. A man could fall in love with Daniela for her cooking alone, though she *looked* as far away from being a chef as he could imagine.

Aldo beamed at him, staying to share a glass of wine, treating him as a favourite customer. At least he was in favour with Daniela's grandad. The mother and father—the Adamis—were an exceptionally good-looking couple but, although charming, weren't quite so warmly welcoming as Aldo. Linc supposed they were wondering about him. Who he was. What he wanted. On the couple of occasions he had called in he must have betrayed his interest in their beautiful daughter.

He was lingering over his coffee when Daniela surprised him by coming to his table. Most of their customers had left by now, expressing very positive comments and indicating they would be coming back.

'You wanted to see me?'

That was the biggest understatement of all time, he thought, overtaken by dense emotion, fierce in its strength.

He stood up immediately, his heart wrenching

yet again as he looked on her beautiful face. There was such grace about her, such refinement, sensitivity, the promise of passion. She was dressed very simply, in a crisp white shirt and black skirt, her lustrous hair clipped back behind her ears.

'I did, as a matter of fact,' he said. 'Could you join me for a minute?' He moved swiftly to hunt up another chair.

'I'm finished for the afternoon,' she said, sitting down and looking up at him—half expectantly, half what? He wasn't sure, but her great eyes glittered. 'So I take it the deal went through?'

He resumed his seat. 'It was settled yesterday. I am now the master of Briar's Ridge.'

'Now, why does that sound like Briar's Ridge is the first in a chain?' she asked.

He was a bit startled. 'I like a challenge.'

'I know you do.'

'More of that woman's intuition?' His eyes locked on hers. 'Don't worry, I'm not knocking it. I have ambitions, Daniela. But you must know all about ambition. You've studied and worked hard. Le Cordon-Bleu, wasn't it, in Paris? Then London? You're rising to the top of your game. And you're what—twenty-four, twenty-five?'

'Does that matter?' She gave an expressive shrug of her delicate shoulders.

'Yes,' he answered bluntly. 'I can tell you I'm twenty-eight, so why can't—'

'Twenty-five,' she supplied. 'It is as you've said. I did have to study and work extremely hard to rise to the top in a very tough business. There was a time when I wanted other things.'

'Like what?' he asked, needing to know.

Her beautiful eyes were distant in thought. 'I wanted to go to university full-time. I was a good student. I could have got into any course I wanted. I was very interested in art history, psychology, the law—oh, lots of things. I wanted to stretch my wings. But there simply wasn't the money. I had to accept that. All of us have had to work hard. We've had to make a go of things. I was needed at home. It was actually an elderly relative who eventually became my benefactor and sent me to Paris. I had four years of schoolgirl French, which was a help. The deal was it had to be food. I was to become a chef.'

'Well, do you enjoy it?' His family had lacked lots of things, but not money.

Her lovely mouth curved in a smile. 'Of course I do. I'm Italian. I'm a woman. You could say my career was clear cut. My benefactor, for instance, wouldn't have advanced the money had I wanted to study Fine Arts.'

'How strange,' he said, thinking it was. 'But

going on the reaction of your lunchtime customers you're a big hit. I was one of them, and what I had was superb.'

She gave a little laugh. 'I can do better. Lots better. I have to consider what our customers would like.'

'So you're telling me I don't know the best?'

'No, no.' She shook her head, looking embarrassed. 'I'm just saying…'

'I know.' He relented.

'You went to university?' She stared at him, unable to help herself. He was almost a stranger, yet she had a real sense of familiarity.

'I have a degree in Economics,' he told her. 'Not entirely useless.' Abruptly he caught hold of her fingertips. He hadn't meant to. It had just happened. 'Who's been cruel to you?'

She tried to withdraw her hand.

He held on. 'Well?' The tormented look on her face stopped him. He let her go.

'This is a mistake, Carl,' she said.

'Please don't go.' He was terrified she would. 'I'm sorry. I came to ask if you would like to see over Briar's Ridge.'

She paused uncertainly. 'What? Out of curiosity?'

'Not at all.' There was a brilliant sparkle in his light eyes, neither silver nor green, but a blend of both. 'There's another reason. I want a woman's opinion. *Your* opinion. You're a smart woman, a woman of taste. The homestead doesn't come with furnishings. I wouldn't want them in any case. I want to start out afresh. I want the place to be my own.'

She studied him strangely. 'How can that be, with *my* taste?'

'To be honest, I believe with you I can't go wrong. You have style. You've had time to acquire sophistication on top of your own inherent polish.'

'You flatter me,' she said. She put up a hand to remove a gold clasp from her hair, so one side went for a silken slide.

He watched in fascination. Everything about her was just so damned romantic, even exotic. 'I don't think so. I'm certainly not trying to.'

'It's a bad time,' she announced, suddenly losing her composure.

'Not a bad time at all. Please—no more excuses, Daniela. Aldo told me you're always free at the weekend. Please say you'll come.'

Again she hesitated. 'You've asked me first?'

He frowned. She seemed to be making some point. 'Who else?'

'I really don't know.' She shook her head, looking as if she had concerns. 'You appeared to be getting along very well with Alana's cousins, Violette and Lilli.'

'So?' He gave her another puzzled frown.

'One of them might be perfect for you,' she said, really looking into his face. 'They come from your world—pastoral families, establishment, that kind of thing.'

He sat back, caught in a moment of empathy. 'I think I'm a lot wiser than that, Daniela. The people I most admire are those who make something of themselves, like you. You have ambition. You're a fighter. You're twenty-five. You haven't stepped back. You've stepped forward. I happen to know Violette and Lilli haven't done a day's work in their lives. In my book even rich girls have to *do* something.'

She began toying with one of the wine glasses. 'Sometimes I'd like to be rich,' she said with a brittle laugh.

'Would you do things differently?'

'What a question!' She stared away.

'Riches don't bring happiness, Daniela. A lot of the time money brings conflict. Anyway, a beautiful young woman like you would find it easy to attract a rich man. He need only *see* you. Maybe one of them did? Maybe he saw you often? It would be normal for you to have many admirers.'

'All these questions,' she said, returning her gaze to him.

'And no answers,' he said crisply. 'Will you come with me tomorrow? I'll pick you up.'

'I need to think about it.' The words implied she wasn't sure if she wanted to see him again. Only he knew differently.

'Okay, that's fine.' He sat back. 'I'm not doing anything in particular.'

She started to run a slender finger around the rim of the unused white wine glass, bringing a certain solemnity to it. 'Tomorrow afternoon,' she said at last.

'I'll pick you up at two?' His gaze pinned hers.

'Yes, two is fine.' She rose with faint agitation, as though if she stayed a moment longer she would change her mind.

At the same time he knew they couldn't get enough of each other.

Either something wonderful would come of it, or nothing good.

After breakfast at the truly excellent Hunter Valley motel where he was staying, Linc hopped in his car and drove out to Briar's Ridge.

A foreman, appointed by Guy, had been left in place to oversee the farm until he took over. Guy had told him he could, if he wished, take on this foreman, whose name was George Rankin. In his fifties George was a gentle giant, quiet but affable, who knew what he was about. George had lived in the valley all his life. He was well known and well liked. A bachelor—he said not by choice, that he had lost his sweetheart to someone else—he and his father had worked a small family property until his father had passed away a year before, after which the property had been sold. George had figured he didn't need much in the way of money, he had enough to see him out, but he quickly found he didn't like a lot of time on his hands. When Guy had offered him part-time work he had jumped at it, and Guy had subsequently shifted him across to Briar's Ridge to work the place until it was sold.

From what Linc had seen of George he did propose to keep him on. Full-time, if George were agreeable. George Rankin was a good man to have on the team. There was a bungalow he could have, so George could live on site as a young aboriginal lad did—Buddy. Alana had told him Buddy came with the place. There had been the sweetest plea in her eyes as she'd said it. It was Buddy's job to look after the stables complex—only two horses remained, but Linc would get more—and generally help out. What had endeared Buddy to Linc was the fact that the young man had taken it upon himself to look after the late Mrs Callaghan's rose garden. To Linc that seemed like an incredibly nice thing to do. For that reason alone he would have allowed Buddy to stay put, but he had also found Buddy to be hard working and reliable—in other words an asset.

Some of the stock had been sold off. The best of the flock—the remainder—came with the property. Linc had plans to expand every which way, and that was why he had taken on a mortgage: use the bank's money while he held on to a good part of his own. He would need it. The homestead—not big, but appealing, with a great view of the rural valley from the upstairs verandah—had to be furnished, and the surrounding gardens had been kept under control. But they needed a woman's hand to work their magic.

When Linc arrived, both George and Buddy were out mustering the woollies, to bring them down into the home paddock. As he looked up to the high ridges he could see their distant figures. The ridges were dominated by the eucalypts—the reason for the marvellous fragrance in the air, a combination of oils and all the dry aromatic scents of the bush. Briar's Ridge had once been one of the nation's premier sheep stations. The Denbys—Alana's family— had been around for ever, since early colonial days. Landed aristocracy with impeccable credentials. His own mother's side of the family, the Lincolns, were descendants of the old squat-tocracy too, but the Mastermanns, although highly regarded, hadn't been in that league. It had been a step up for his dad to marry a Lincoln. It had given him the seal of establish-ment approval.

Guy, as a Radcliffe, had always had it. The historic station he had inherited usually cleaned up all the competition in the wool sales. He had seen stacks of Grand Champion Fleece ribbons in Guy's study. Wangaree fleece was as white as snow and superfine. Everyone in the business knew the big overseas fashion houses showed enormous interest in it.

It was going to be tough for Linc. Sheep farming was a costly business, and the man on the land always had to contend with drought. Still, he knew he was up to it. It wouldn't be too long and he would be winning awards in his own right. He had won them for Gilgarra, of course. Chuck had helped, too, but their dad had taken all the credit. He'd have to get himself a couple of really good sheep dogs. A really good dog could work a couple of thousand sheep. He, like Alana, favoured Border Collies. Guy had pointed him in the right direction, but he would need to train them *his* way. He loved dogs. He loved animals. Sometimes he thought more than people.

It was very quiet, very peaceful, except for the birds flying through the air or diving ecstatically into the nectar-filled wilderness. This was the first time he had visited Briar's Ridge on his own. Now it was *his*. It gave him a sense of accomplishment and fresh purpose. He hunted up the right key, unlocking the front door. Cleaners had been in. Everything was spick and span. Slowly he walked through the empty rooms, his mind already outlining what steps towards renovation he would take. Guy had given him the names of tradesmen who worked in the area—carpenters, painters, plasterers, tilers, electricians and so forth. This wasn't a grand house like Wangaree, and it didn't approach Gilgarra homestead either, but he was eager to put his own stamp on it. His boots were making quite a clatter on the polished floors—a bright yellow-gold, Queensland maple, he thought. He liked polished timber. It made a nice contrast with the pale walls. He would, however, need rugs…

He fancied his mother's presence went with him. Strangely, it was a lovely feeling instead of sad. She was never far away. He made a leisurely inspection of the ground floor, all the while with ideas flitting through his mind. He liked the proportions of the rooms. The kitchen probably needed a total make-over, but there was no real hurry. It was quite adequate as it was. Indeed, it was great to have absolute freedom and not have to dodge an over-sexed stepmother.

The golden timber staircase led to the second floor, where four of the bedrooms—there were five—were strung along the rear of the house, affording a splendid view of rolling hills and the broad valley. He walked out onto the verandah, resting his hands on the timber railing, drinking it in. The country wasn't as lush and green as he was used to in New England, close as it was to tropical Queensland, this area had the dryness of the bush. But there was a small creek that wound its way through the property. Its waters flashed silver in the brilliant sunlight. He wouldn't have much trouble adapting here.

He had asked Daniela because he wanted, *needed*, to see her. He hadn't the slightest doubt she would come up with ideas that would please him—that was if she was interested in pleasing him—but her presence was what he really wanted. He knew something about houses. He had always been interested in them. He wasn't about to change anything that didn't need changing—he needed to address its country feel—but he had already got a list going in his head.

Some time around ten he had a chat with

George and Buddy. Both looked pleased to see him. He asked Buddy what he was planning to do that afternoon.

'Have fun, Boss!' Buddy gave his big engaging grin.

'Well, you'll be needing your wages, then,' Linc said, withdrawing two envelopes from his shirt pocket.

'That's okay, Boss.' Buddy threw up his hands. 'Mr Radcliffe paid us.'

George twitched the broad brim of his hat. 'That's right,' he agreed gruffly, his leathery face burning with what looked like embarrassment.

'Well, it's all official now,' Linc said. 'I'm the new owner. I'm paying you in advance.'

'Yeah?' Buddy gave a smile. 'That's great. I'm planning on having a big dinner in town. Maybe that Italian place. Everyone reckons it's tops.'

'What about you, George?' Linc asked, passing each of them an envelope.

'I'll just roam around.' George coloured hotly. 'Tonight I'm having dinner with some of my folks. My eldest sister Joyce and her husband. Joycie always tries to be kind.'

Should one have to *try*? Linc thought, divining the depth of the man's loneliness.

Buddy had opened his envelope. Now he was looking overjoyed. 'Did you check this, Boss?' he asked breathlessly, as though Linc might have made a mistake.

'I did, Buddy.' Linc nodded. 'You're on a man's wage from now on.'

'He earns it.' George gripped Buddy's shoulder tight. Buddy had been a big help that morning.

'Well, off you go, Buddy,' Linc said. 'Have a nice day.'

'You, too, Boss.' Buddy all but danced away. 'See yah, G!'

Linc gave an amused chuckle, then turned back to his foreman. 'I wanted to have a private word with you, George.'

George threw up his big weatherbeaten hands. 'That's okay—you got someone else.' He had leapt to the wrong conclusion.

Linc shook his head. 'That's not what I was going to say. I'd like to keep you on full-time, George, if you're agreeable. I even thought you might like to live on the property, like Buddy. There's that little bungalow near the creek that's standing vacant. I've had a look at it. A lick of paint, a few furnishings and it could be made very comfortable. What do you say?'

George took a deep breath, staring up at a flight of pink and pearl-grey galahs. He sighed heavily.

'No problem if you want to stay in town,

George,' Linc said. 'I just thought it might make it easier all round?'

More silence. George took another deep breath, like a man in a haze. Linc was starting to think George couldn't quite believe what was being offered.

'If you'd like to think it over first…?' he suggested.

'Hell, no!' George came suddenly alive. 'It's very good of you to offer. The bungalow would suit me fine. I'd like that.'

'Hey, George, this will suit *me* as well as you,' Linc pointed out with a smile. 'I'll open some accounts in town—the hardware store first up. You can buy all you need. Paint, brushes, whatever.'

George's eyes had turned inward. 'I've got plenty of furniture stored,' he announced, his dour face so bright he looked years younger.

'Then it's all settled.' Linc held out his hand. 'Better check your wages.'

'They'll be fine.' George slapped his thigh. His expression said it all. He liked and trusted Linc.

'Well, then…' Linc held out his hand. George took it.

'Welcome home, Mr Mastermann,' he said.

'Linc.' Linc waved the 'Mr Mastermann' away. 'Only my dad gets called Mr Mastermann,

George. Though I don't mind Buddy calling me Boss. He gets a kick out of it, anyway.'

'He's a good lad. I can teach him a lot,' George said. 'Anything against my moving in by next weekend?' George wasn't going to admit it, but he found town life depressing.

'No problem.' Linc started to turn away. 'Oh, and Buddy might like to give you a hand with the bungalow?'

George was too jammed up with emotion to reply.

CHAPTER FOUR

HE DROVE her to Briar's Ridge and she hardly spoke a word for the first few minutes, looking out of the window as they made a smooth exit from town.

'This is a beautiful car,' she said appreciatively. 'It suits you.'

He gave an ironic laugh. 'You think so? I inherited the Lincoln passion for fast cars. My dad said it was a bad choice. He made it sound like *me*.'

'You and your father are not good friends, then?' she asked, turning her head to study his handsome, clean-cut profile.

'I don't think we ever were,' he muttered, almost to himself. 'It's always been a kind of confrontational relationship.'

'Your temperaments clash?'

His voice firmed. 'That's one form it takes.'

'What's another?'

He shrugged. 'My father is a tough, aggressive man, yet I seem to make him feel threatened. I don't know why that is. I've done nothing to make him feel like that. He gets on a whole lot better with Chuck—that's my brother, Charles. Dad abandoned the "Charles" very early in the peace. Chuck was named in honour of my grandfather— my maternal grandfather—a real gentleman of Guy Radcliffe's mould. Dad always tended to resent my mother's family as being a bit too grand when really they couldn't have been kinder or more generous.'

'Then how did your father win your mother's hand?'

He took a left, driving off the highway. In a grassy paddock two beautiful horses were racing each other around the perimeter, a bright chestnut and a glossy bay, manes and tails flying, a glorious sight. The car rode on seamlessly, as though it already knew the route by heart. A quarter of a mile on was the main thoroughfare that wound through the valley.

'Obviously I wasn't there at the time, but I think he played a loving role for as long as he had to. My mother was a beautiful woman—very gentle, very feminine. To be honest, I don't know *how* she got involved with my father. They didn't have a thing in common.'

'Outside sexual attraction?'

His laugh was dark-edged. 'That's the danger

of sexual attraction, isn't it? If that's all you've got, a marriage mightn't have much of a chance. In time I guess passion banks. Maybe affection was always lacking? Disappointment and disillusionment were bound to set in.'

She looked at him in a searching way. 'My parents and my grandparents share much love.'

'Then you've been blessed,' he said shortly, his grip firming on the wheel as they took a sharp curve.

'I know.'

'You have no siblings?'

'I'm an only child. My parents wanted—prayed for more. But it was not to be.'

'Well, they got a one-off.' He glanced at her with a taut smile.

She was wearing a very pretty silk blouse, sunshine-yellow with little wings for sleeves, over cream linen trousers. The decorative gold buckle of her belt matched the half-dozen thin bracelets she wore on her right hand. She had a real feel for style. He was sure it was innate.

'As a child I missed not having a brother or sister,' she said. 'I had to deal with the question of identity as a first- generation Australian.'

He turned his head swiftly. 'You surely didn't have a bad time?'

'No.' She looked out at the surrounding countryside with its stands of banksia, urn-fruited peppermint and scribbly gums. 'A good time, really. Maybe at first there were difficulties. My family spoke a different first language, and I had acquired an accent, but I was bilingual. My grandmother to this day doesn't speak good English. And we looked different. We ate different food. We were Europeans, as opposed to the migrant families from the British Isles. They fitted in naturally. Most of the population is of British descent anyway. Those of us from the Mediterranean seemed to be cut off from the old home. But gradually I found my way and I became popular.'

'All you needed was to be yourself. I understand the difficulties,' he said. 'But I sense it has made you stronger. And there have been huge changes. You will have seen that yourself. Australia embraces its cultural mix.'

'Didn't someone say if you speak like an Aussie, you *are* an Aussie?'

He laughed quietly. 'Were you happier in London?'

She hesitated. 'I lived another sort of life there. London is a great city. It taught me much. But, like all ex-pats, I'm glad to be home.'

'You had problems there.'

It wasn't a question. She turned her lustrous head away, thinking he was too good at mind-reading. 'Don't we all have problems? I would have thought with your family background you would have wished to remain close to home. Yours is a working station—an important one, I understand. Or will your brother as the firstborn son inherit? You haven't spoken of any other family members?'

'That's because there's just Chuck and me. And of course Cheryl.' He had to struggle to keep out the derisive note. 'Dad is as fit as a fiddle—a big, strong, handsome man—but Gilgarra will eventually pass to both of us. The only reason for that is because Lincoln money really put Gilgarra on the map. I'm part of the deal. My mother looked after both her boys.'

'But you were the favourite?' She caught his silver-green eyes. 'There's always one.'

'If I was my mother didn't show it. At least I don't think she did. In any case, Dad favoured Chuck.'

'And who does your stepmother favour?'

'I hope you're not looking for an answer, Daniela?' He gave her a swift, sidelong glance, cool and sizzling at the same time.

She knew it was an incautious question, but she couldn't seem to help herself. 'So you thought striking out on your own was the best policy?'

'I should have done it years ago, but Dad really needed me. Gilgarra needed me.'

'Your father and Chuck can't do the job on their own?'

'They're going to have to,' he said. 'Are you finished with the questions?'

'For the time being,' she said lightly. Nothing could subdue the dangerous sense of excitement that shimmered between them.

She didn't see the homestead until they had broken out of the luminous green and gold speckled light beneath the crossed arms of sentinel trees. Then the broad circular driveway welcomed them, its fine gravel a dazzling white under the hot sun.

The word that immediately sprang to Daniela's mind for the homestead and its setting was an old one—picturesque. She sensed that for many years it had been a happy place. Alana had told her her mother had been killed in a tragic car crash with her father at the wheel. That would have been an awful lot of grief to contend with. Since then she had learned Alana's father had never thrown off an unwarranted sense of guilt. It appeared that guilt in the end had become too much for him.

She had taken for granted she was the only person Carl had invited, but a young woman was there before them. Lilli Denby. She was leaning back against the side of a silver Mercedes sports car, looking for all the world like a top model on a shoot. As they approached she made a move away from it, dropping her turquoise shoulder bag to the ground. It was impossible to tell if Lilli looked pleased Linc had a female with him. Lilli was wearing designer sunglasses with big black lenses, a stylish floppy-brimmed white hat on her blond head. A very trendy turquoise, black and white trapeze dress skimmed her ultra-slim body. Turquoise sandals were on her feet.

'It looks like your friend Lilli beat us to it.' Daniela spoke casually even though she was shrinking inside. She hadn't taken to two out of the three Denby sisters—Alana's cousins. Rose, the youngest, was by far the nicest, but Rose's two elder sisters had come across as incredibly snobbish. 'You might have told me she'd be here as well.'

'Oh, that?' he remarked dryly. 'The thing is Lilli neglected to tell *me*. You know perfectly well I didn't invite her.'

'That's okay. I believe you. You may well not have invited her *today*.' Going on what she had witnessed at the wedding, women threw themselves at him. It made her shiver. 'The wedding was obviously the start of a beautiful friendship.'

He glanced at her, a glint of amusement in his cool silver-green eyes. 'I promise she won't stay long.'

They all stood out in the dazzling sunlight. A flight of brilliantly plumaged lorikeets flew through the iridescent air, heading for the wealth of nectar-bearing grevilleas. 'Hello there, Lilli,' Linc called in his dark-timbred sexy voice. 'You're looking for me?'

'Who else?' she responded, with a sexy lilt of her own. 'I was on my way into town, so I thought I'd stop on the off-chance you were here.'

'You were lucky.' Linc smiled down at her, his deep dimples coming into play. 'The property was only settled yesterday.'

'I know.' She whipped off her sunglasses to give him an 'insider' smirk.

'Really? It wasn't exactly front-page news.'

Lilli's big blue eyes sparkled. 'We Denbys have our sources.'

He'd already learned that. The Denbys were an old family, but as far as he could gauge not terribly well liked. 'You know Daniela, of course.' Linc turned his head towards Daniela, standing so quietly.

Now Lilli's gaze held outright condescension. 'Didn't we meet at Guy's wedding?' She frowned, as though to place Daniela. 'Ah, yes! You work at your family's little bistro in town, don't you?'

'Let's just say I'm helping out,' Daniela answered with composure. Over the years she had met many women more arrogant than Lilli, and heaps further up the social scale.

'We must try to pop in some time,' Lilli said, as

though the experience would amuse her. Immediately she turned back to Linc. 'Any chance of seeing through the house?' She twisted an arm through his.

'You're joking?' he scoffed. 'You must have been here countless times, what with Alana and Kieran being your cousins?'

Lilli gave a little grimace. 'Actually, while their dad was alive we stayed away. He wasn't the easiest man in the world. Quite the rough diamond, in fact. It was Alana's mother who was the Denby. Surely Guy told you?'

Daniela felt herself cringe at the snobbery and tried to disguise it.

Linc's answer was level enough. 'He didn't get into bloodlines, Lilli. It was Alana who told me you and your sisters are her first cousins. So how long is it since you've been here?'

Lilli hooted. 'Too long to tell. I'm sure you're going to want to do the place up?' She controlled a splutter of laughter, as though the homestead was all but falling down. 'Perhaps give a house-warming party? Is that why Ms Adami is here?'

Linc shook his curly raven head. 'Daniela is here at my invitation.'

Lilli picked up quickly on the steely note in his voice. 'Ouch!' She gave a tiny mock screech. 'No offence, Daniela.'

'None taken.' Daniela inclined her elegant head. 'I've handled many a housewarming party over the last few years.' She could have dropped a few world celebrity names, but she didn't. Her clients trusted her—and her discretion.

'Well, shall we go inside?' Linc put a good face on it. It was just impossible to get rid of Lilli, he thought. She had a remarkably thick skin. More than anything he had wanted Daniela to be the first one he showed over Briar's Ridge, but now Lilli had made her move. In a way she reminded him a bit of Cheryl. Cheryl, too, liked to take the initiative.

Lilli stayed perhaps thirty minutes, prodding Linc in the chest as she pointed out an endless list of things she considered had to be done. Not a room escaped criticism, nor he her little prods, accompanied by some sort of complicit grin. Daniela might not have been there for all Lilli included her in the conversation.

'Lilli, if you're interested you're going to leave me black and blue,' Linc said, not altogether in jest.

'A big strong guy like you?' She eyed him appreciatively from head to toe.

Lilli was definitely interested, Daniela thought. She would have found out all she needed to know about Linc Mastermann—a few comments from Guy, the rest on the pastoral grapevine. Neither

Violette nor Lilli was currently in a steady relationship, she understood from Alana. She thought of
Alana with nostalgia. She was a wonderful young
woman, as lovely inside as out. So far as her cousins
were concerned, Linc Mastermann must have
appeared on the scene like God's gift to women.

'Can I give you a lift back into town, Daniela?'
Lilli asked, suddenly remembering she was there.
'I can easily drop you off at the coffee shop.'
Obviously she thought shoving Daniela down the
social scale was the way to go.

'There are a few more things I want Daniela to
see,' Linc intervened.

A lengthy pause. 'Okay,' Lilli managed, her
sparkle visibly dimmed. 'How long are you
staying in town?' she asked Daniela. It wasn't
conversation. She really wanted to know. 'A
country town can't be much fun after London.
Alana told me something about your career.
You're a cook, aren't you?'

'Wake up, Lilli,' Linc drawled, thinking this
had gone far enough, although Daniela didn't
appear in the least bothered. 'The word is *chef*.
Daniela has made it to the top of the tree.'

Lilli's laugh fell a little flat. 'It's great you're
interested in such a career.' She made it sound an
unacceptable one. 'I would have thought it would
be very tough going, even dangerous, with all

those sharp knives around and those volatile temperaments. I can't even boil an egg.'

'Why do eggs figure so largely on the "can't manage" list?' Daniela laughed. 'You'd soon learn if you didn't have someone to do things for you.'

'Actually, I've better things to do with my time,' Lilli trilled. 'Could you walk me out to my car, Linc?' she asked, training her blue eyes on him.

'Sure.' Lean cheeks creased in a smile.

Lilli interpreted that as a very good sign. She tethered herself to his arm.

No question—Lilli Denby had Linc Mastermann well and truly in her sights.

Left alone, Daniela brooded for a moment only. What am I doing here? she thought. I've fled one bad situation. I'd be crazy to walk into another.

Perhaps you're a little jealous of Lilli? asked a voice in her head.

She rejected that. She didn't blame Lilli for being so powerfully attracted to him. She was herself. But she wasn't going to let it go to her head. She had always prided herself on her common sense. Yet wasn't it true she'd been the last one to know Gerald Templeton had developed an intense fixation on her? In the early days she'd thought—if she'd bothered to think about it at all—that he fancied her.

It had been something of a joke with the other

staff, but she had always kept her distance from customers—even when she and Tim, her talented offsider, had catered for the rich and famous. Besides, Gerald wasn't the only man who had endeavoured not only to chat her up but to ask her out. Eventually she had accepted one of Gerald's dinner invitations. It had gone well. He was good-looking, of good family, highly educated, clever. In short, a real catch. They had talked aimlessly and pleasantly about art, the theatre, books, people, travel, although she had steered clear of talking about his circle of friends who came frequently to the restaurant. Gerald was very much the man about town, with enviable connections.

Nothing dramatic had happened for quite a while. He'd taken her to lots of places, and she had even met his parents, at their beautiful country home—though not in a formal, girlfriend-meeting-the-parents sort of way. The young women of Gerald's circle always came from his own world. But what had started out in such a pleasant civilised fashion had turned into something else. It had grown darker and darker until she had fled.

'Daniela?'

Carl's voice pulled her out of her troubled thoughts. 'Carl?' Somehow Carl seemed more natural to her than *Linc*. She turned. 'Back again?'

He laughed briefly, something inside him tightening at the use of his real first name. He wasn't going to stop her. Maybe he even had a fierce necessity of the heart to hear his Christian name again? 'Do you think there was a damned thing Lilli *didn't* want to change? Next time she might come with a tape measure and take notes.'

'So there's going to *be* a next time?' She shot him a wry look.

He met those lustrous dark eyes. 'Tell me, is there a way to prevent it?' It was said with amusement, but a lick of bitterness escaped, too. It wasn't only men who did the chasing.

'I can only say Lilli appears to find you special.'

'Put it down to New Man in Town syndrome,' he returned.

'So modest? I think Lilli and her sister Violette meet plenty of men. They're on the social circuit, and both of them spend a lot of time in Sydney and Melbourne. Violette even implied she and Guy were once an item.'

'That must have been before Alana.' Linc spoke very dryly.

She nodded her strong agreement. 'I'd say so. I've never seen two people so much in love.'

They moved slowly into the large living area, with its pairs of French doors, shuttered on the outside, opening onto the wide covered verandah that offered refuge from the intensity of the sun.

'So how did you meet Alana?' he asked. 'Your face lights up when you talk about her.'

'I imagine a lot of people's faces light up around Alana,' Daniela said with a smile. 'She's a lovely person. Very endearing. No guile. No side. And she wears her beauty so gracefully.'

'As do you,' he said, allowing his eyes to feast on her.

She took in a deep, slow breath, not answering. The truth was she was feeling the intense heat of his masculinity—the height, the shape of him, the width of shoulder that tapered away to a narrow waist, lean hips, long legs. His aura was so magnetic she felt she had to stand a distance from him, just as she needed to stand a distance from her own emotions. She had never imagined anything so explosive as the effect Carl Mastermann was having on her.

'I think I need platforms around you.' She tried a joke, tilting her head as though it hurt her to look up at him.

He laughed, glancing down at her sandalled feet. 'I'd feel bad if you toppled over. So, how did you meet Alana?' he reminded her.

Daniela walked a few paces to the next set of doors, looking out. A bird was singing in the garden, its song plaintive but very sweet. She thought the sound came from an ornamental tree with a thick circle of pink flowers beneath it. 'She and her cousin Rose came into the bistro about a week after I arrived home. We got talking. You could say we were immediately drawn to each other. I like Rose as well—she has a sweeter nature than her sisters—but Alana is my clear favourite. We met up a number of times after that. And of course I had to meet her wonderful Guy. It was easy to see why Alana fell in love with him. Guy was very interested in the fact I had a couple of Cordon Bleu diplomas, and I'd worked in London's top restaurants. I've been to his Winery Restaurant and met the chef. He's extremely good. He'd get a top job anywhere. Guy was keen on sounding me out—whether I'd ever be interested in taking over the running of the Winery Restaurant at some time in the future. The money he was talking was certainly an inducement. I understand the chef has been there a good while and regularly gets tempting offers from all over—especially Hong Kong, where he has family. I got the impression there was a good chance he might move on.'

'Would you consider it if that happened?' Linc asked, his mind flying to what that would mean.

'I can't think that far ahead,' she said evasively, though in actuality she *had* thought about it.

'Really?' He had his own trip wire to the truth. 'It sounds to me like you've given Guy's offer a lot of thought. I could be wrong, but I don't think you have a mind to return to London any time soon. Did you quit your job?'

She continued to stare out at the shimmering dreamscape. The heat was like a pulsing white fire. A fountain would look lovely in the centre of the driveway, she thought. One always needed a fountain in this kind of dry heat.

'I've taken leave,' she said, not altogether truthfully.

'If you took the job at Guy's would you feel you had taken a step backwards in your career?' he asked, fully understanding that she might. 'After all, London is one of the great cities of the world— a far cry from the Hunter Valley.'

She turned to face him, a sudden flash in her dark eyes. 'You're forgetting I love my country. My family is here. I love everything about Australia—the peace and freedom, the friendliness, our whole way of life and for God's sake the *climate*! It's claimed not many Australians can settle in a cold, wet climate, and I believe it. Don't forget I'm also Italian.'

'I realised that right off.' He gave her his dimpled smile.

'Couldn't miss it.' She shrugged wryly. She

would never hide her Italian heritage. She had no wish to. She was proud of it. 'What you mightn't be aware of is that Australia has some very important chefs, food writers and teachers. All of them have done stints in London and elsewhere. But in my view Australians can dine as well as anyone for a whole lot less, with the finest natural ingredients readily to hand, especially seafood.'

He admired her enthusiasm. 'So now we've got that sorted out. Anyway, I wasn't about to give you an argument. I've done my share of travelling.'

'But your roots are here?'

He extended his long arms as though to encompass his world. 'I have this amazing idea I'm going to start a dynasty of my own.'

She could see he was serious. 'Then I wish you every success. But you'll need a wife to bear your children, and before you marry you should consult your future wife about your plans for this dynasty. What did you have in mind? Twenty children, like Johann Sebastian Bach?'

He laughed. 'Four should be enough. And I think you'll find Herr Bach fathered all those children by two different women.'

'I knew that,' she replied, a tiny bit surprised that he did, too.

'So you want to marry, have children? Or are you a career woman?'

'I have to find a man I can love first,' she said, weaving her way elegantly around the living room.

'*Can* love? You sound a tad off men.'

'Good! You're learning that early,' she commented, moving into what would be the dining room.

'Okay, you're complicated. I understand complicated.'

They exchanged a brief glance. 'Both of us appear to have unresolved conflicts.' There was a brittle edge to Daniela's voice she couldn't control.

'Why do you want to keep yours secret?' He could see the struggle on her beautiful face.

'Carl, I don't know you.' She paused, her accent suddenly more pronounced. 'Not well, anyway. And I'm not the only one with secrets. There are things *you* don't want to talk about.'

'That's true.' He watched her stroke back a thick strand of hair that seemed to give off its own light. 'I like to keep a distance from my own emotions. Yours seem to be right there. I can't pretend I don't see your bruises.'

He had an uncanny knack to go to the heart of things. 'On my arms? Where?' She reacted sharply, turning out her slender arms, pretending to inspect her glowing golden skin. 'I see no bruises.'

'They're all inside. Okay—I can see it's necessary to change the subject, get onto something safe. Why don't we go through the house again now that Lilli has said her reluctant goodbyes?'

She stood framed by an open white timber archway. 'It seems a shame to waste her suggestions. Sorry, I didn't mean that.' She detested herself for sounding a touch cruel.

He laughed. 'I think really she wanted the house knocked down. I'm desperate to hear from *you*. I'm not going in for grandeur, like Wangaree. A laid-back style of living is what I have in mind. This is a country homestead.'

She nodded. 'But you'll want it to be comfortable and attractive, light and airy, a happy, welcoming place. I'd suggest a few unusual, possibly unique things. A light palette for the walls and furnishings. That should integrate the rooms. Thai furniture would work well, don't you think? Surely you brought things back from your travels?'

He studied her petite figure in an unabashedly sensual, brooding way. Being with her alone was making it hard to keep his attraction to her in check. 'As a matter of fact I did—especially from Southeast Asia. I've always been drawn to Balinese and Asian artifacts and antiques.'

'A touch of the exotic?' She smiled. It was a beautiful smile, glowing. That didn't make it easy for him either.

Did she have the faintest idea how much he

wanted to kiss her? Only the last thing he needed was to fracture what was at the moment a fragile relationship. More to the point, he didn't want to spook her. He could see someone in her not too distant past had already done that. He found he hated the thought—hated the guy.

'I have quite a lot of stuff stored at Gilgarra. I can get Chuck to send it to me.'

'You don't want to go back and get it?' She, too, was picking up on the vibes.

'No,' he said briefly.

She walked towards the filmy curtains that had been left in place, putting out a hand to finger them. 'What about white interior shutters instead of curtains?' she suggested. 'They could look good— control the light—and you wouldn't have to worry about constantly getting the curtains washed. I love the polished floors. I love that dark honey colour. But you'll need rugs and a few paintings—prints, botanical or ornithological, whatever.'

'Your vision is pretty well the same as mine,' he said with satisfaction. 'Let's go upstairs,' he said, doing a slow turn and extending his arm. 'The master bedroom is a good size. I'll settle for that for myself.' He waited for her to precede him.

Neither of them spoke again until they were inside the spacious main bedroom. Daniela looked about her. 'I really like this room,' she said. 'It has a very serene feeling and the view is wonderfully soothing. You could easily fit in a huge bed— maybe Balinese, custom-made for your height. I see it already. Sofa, tub armchairs, low table, carved chest at the foot of the bed. And I'd change the ceiling fan to fit the décor you work out.'

She walked past him out onto the verandah, staring out at the marvellously peaceful view. Linc followed.

'This is magnificent!' She lifted a radiant face, breathing in the fragrant aromatic air. 'You have it first thing in the morning, last thing at night. Nothing and no one to spoil it. I love the smell of the eucalypts.'

'So do I,' Linc said. 'But we can never forget their fire danger. The oil is highly inflammable and it hangs in the air. Fires have broken out up there from time to time, so I'll be on high alert from now on in. I've always been strict on fire pre-vention methods. I'll be much stricter here than we ever were in the New England highlands.'

'So what do you intend to do?' Born and bred in Sydney, Daniela had little knowledge of rural life— apart from recognising that for all the rewards it was very tough, to the point of heartbreaking.

'Plough firebreaks around the perimeter of the property,' Linc told her. 'It mightn't be all that popular in some quarters, but with global warming!' He shrugged. 'Some superfine farmers don't like the dust in the air. It gets into the fleece and dirties the wool. I certainly don't want to do it—it will be one hell of a task, given the size of the place—but it has to be done. We've missed out on the spring rains, and last year the fire season started early in the Southern Highlands, around the Hawkesbury and the Hunter Valley regions. Major drought always brings the threat of severe bushfires. It's in everyone's minds. The end of last year—you wouldn't have been back in Australia then—bushfires raged in the Blue Mountains.'

'I did see some TV coverage,' she said. 'And I heard all about it from the family. The most horrifying aspect is that some of the fires were lit by arsonists.'

'They're murderers,' Linc said starkly. 'They seem to rejoice in death and destruction.' He reined his tone back. God help any pyromaniac who got onto *his* property. 'There's a great Rural Fire Service in the valley. I made it my business to meet up with them.'

'So you'll be well prepared?'

'As much as I can be,' he said. 'With bushfires, all the wildlife in the hills suffer. If the fires eventually sweep down into the valley we'll lose stock, but hopefully no lives.'

'There must be lots of wallabies and kangaroos up there?' She looked towards the rolling hills that stood watch over the station.

'Bound to be. Wallabies, kangaroos, possums, bandicoots, snakes and lizards, wedge-tailed and whistling eagles, lyrebirds and a phenomenal number of parrots. I plan on making a trek into the hill country some time soon. Want to come when I do?'

They were standing quite close. Too close. Hands spread on the balustrade, little fingers almost touching.

'Go up into the hills with you?' She felt a frisson of something like alarm. How could she possibly put herself in the way of temptation?

'No need to make it sound like a foreign country. You haven't been in hill country before?'

'I haven't been in the bush before,' she said wryly. 'I lived all my life in Sydney, forever drawn to the beach. The bird life here is wonderful, isn't it? They shriek, whistle, sing, and they're hardly invisible. I've never seen so many brilliant colours.' As she spoke another wave of rainbow lorikeets, flashing their showy plumage, dived into a blossoming stand of bauhinias. 'So many things in the garden are fruiting and flowering. I envy you, Carl. You can do such a lot with this place.'

'And I intend to do just that,' he said, pleased

by her reactions. 'When we go up into the hills we'll have to get you a sleeping bag. You can discover the stars. In the wild bush they're so big and beautiful, so *close* they could be hanging from the branches of the trees. Can you ride?'

She shook her head with regret. 'The only horses I've been anywhere close to have been at the races.'

'You're not frightened of them?'

She laughed that away. 'No. Horses have to be the most beautiful of animals.'

'Then I can easily teach you.'

She was caught completely off guard. 'Why would you want to? Why do you want to take me with you up into the hill country?' She turned to face him fully.

'I think you know the answer to that,' he said. 'Shall we go through the other bedrooms?'

'Yes, of course.'

Whatever was between them, it was happening fast.

As soon as Lilli arrived home she went in search of her older sister. She was much closer to Violette than she was to Rose, who in any case was at work at the Radcliffe Estates Winery.

It rather amused the family that Rose was holding down a job. They were all in agreement that it was because it enabled her to come into daily contact with the young man she had long fancied herself in love with—Simon Radcliffe, Guy's cousin. That fact of his name alone ensured Simon was looked on favourably by the family. Simon had a dragon of a mother, but little butter-wouldn't-melt-in-her-mouth Rose seemed to be handling her surprisingly well.

Rose and Simon had been going steady for some time, and the family supposed they would soon announce their engagement. But Lilli and Violette were not getting any younger, and were no closer to finding suitable husbands. Both of them had had relationships, and Violette had seri-ously believed Guy would eventually get around to asking her to marry him—heritage families stuck together—but that had never happened. Alana had scooped the prize. Now Guy's friend, Linc Mastermann, had moved into the valley. Both she and Violette had been instantly at-tracted. This was one sexy guy. Better yet, on their social level.

She just *knew* Linc was going places. He had that air about him. Just as she knew that close sisters both being attracted to the same man might cause trouble. Privately she considered Linc had found *her* the more appealing. The last thing she had expected was to find someone else who might be ahead of them. She needed to alert Vi before a situation developed...

Violette was in her bedroom, trying on a new evening dress in her favourite shade of electric blue.

'What do you think?' Violette twirled for her sister's inspection.

'Gorgeous! You'll definitely score in that one.'

'And I know exactly *who* I have my eye on,' Violette chortled, running her hands caressingly down over her ultra slim hips.

'I have to tell you someone else has her eye on him,' she said bluntly, flopping down in an armchair.

'Who are we talking about, *exactly*?' Violette unzipped herself, at the same time aiming a piercing glance at her sister.

'Well, we're both keen on Linc...'

Violette gave a little inelegant snort. 'Darling, *you* should be so lucky! We both know he fancies *me*.'

'I don't know that at all.' Petulantly, Lilli swung a slender leg. Violette never let her forget who the big sister was.

'Yeah, well, I need to get married before *you*,' Violette reminded her. 'And Linc Mastermann is the only one I'd consider after Guy. He's drop-dead sexy.'

'Dreamy!' Lilli agreed. 'Only that Italian chick—the one from the bistro—thinks so, too.'

Violette looked dumbstruck. 'Italian chick? Should that mean something to me?'

Lilli gave a sly smirk. 'Ah, come off it! You know—the *bellissima* one at the wedding. Alana's latest friend.'

'Hell!' Violette pitched her evening gown onto her four-poster before swivelling towards her sister. 'How do you know? Anyway, isn't she a *chef* or something?' She made it sound like a kennel maid.

'She must be the only chef around who doesn't like food,' Lilli lamented. She and Violette had to work very hard to keep their admittedly great figures, while Miss Italy, who just *had* to be sampling what she turned out, was a perfect pocket Venus.

Violette pulled a white tank top down over her head, sounding thoroughly rattled. 'What would be the point of her getting interested in Linc when she's only here to see her family? She'll be back in London before we know it.'

'I don't know about that,' Lilli muttered doubtfully. 'I think she's a teeny weeny bit in love with him already. That could make a *huge* difference.'

'In love with him?' Violette questioned grimly.

'Are you going to repeat everything after me?' Lilli asked, quite crossly. 'Look, I don't *know*… but you know what Dad says: forewarned is forearmed. I was just passing Briar's Ridge—'

'You were *passing* Briar's Ridge?' Violette cried scornfully. 'You mean you went right out of your way. You've got to put a stop to going behind my back, Lilli,' she warned wrathfully.

Lilli cleared her throat. 'As far as I'm concerned, it's every man for himself. You know what they say, Vi. All's fair in love and war.'

'You get between me and Linc and I'll squeeze the life out of you,' Violette said, making strangling motions with her long-fingered hands.

Lilli groaned in disgust. 'We're sisters, remember. *Family!*'

'To hell with that! You're not trying to tell me *she* was there?'

Lilli shrugged. 'I arrived first. They arrived about ten minutes later. He'd brought her out to show her around the place. He took us both on a tour.'

'Only he *invited* her,' said Violette, bitterly sarcastic. 'You invited yourself.'

'Unfair, isn't it?' Lilli sighed. 'And I have to say she looks really high class. I just thought I should let you know.'

'And maybe I'll get around to thanking you one of these days. No way I'm going to take this lying down.' Violette turned to stare at herself in a mirror, almost blinded by her own beauty. She was definitely the pick of the three beautiful Denby sisters.

'Maybe he thinks flirting is just a bit of a game?' Lilli suggested. 'At the wedding he seemed taken with both of *us*. Then again, maybe we were the ones doing the flirting. And he was just playing up to us. That's the trouble with sexy guys. They play up to us girls.'

Violette turned away from her self-adoration. She had already considered her move. 'What do you say we call in on this outsider at her place of business? Do lunch one day? Her aim is way off if she thinks she's got a chance of bagging Linc Mastermann.'

'If anyone can put her in her place, Vi, it's you,' Lilli said loyally, even though she had some private doubts.

'Easy-peasy.' Violette nodded a petulant agreement. 'And I think you mean *Violette*.'

CHAPTER FIVE

IN THE car, he was aware her lovely body was tense beside him. Tree branches above them loomed over the car like a shadowy canopy. Both of them had got under each other's skin. It was exciting, but not the most relaxed feeling in the world.

She looked sideways at him. 'Thank you, Carl, for asking me. I enjoyed that.'

'Then maybe you'll enjoy having dinner with me tonight?' he said, briefly pinning her dark gaze. 'And don't tell me you have to work, because I know you don't. I have your grandfather on side.'

'It would seem so,' she admitted wryly. 'But haven't we seen enough of each other for one day?'

He was quiet a while. 'You want to fight the attraction?'

'You're certain there *is* one?' There was a soft little ache in her voice.

'You are, too.'

By now she was resigned to it. 'But neither of us are relaxed about it.'

'No.' He answered without looking at her. He didn't feel he could absorb much more of her beauty before he stopped the car and reached for her. Could never get enough of her.

'Have you ever been in love? I mean *really* in love?' she asked, sounding to Linc's ears as though she actually cared. 'Putting someone above yourself?'

He took a moment to consider. 'Desire flares up suddenly, and often just as suddenly dies down. I've had some very pleasant relationships—and I certainly hope I haven't done any woman any harm—but I haven't had a relationship serious enough to study it in any depth.' Usually he deliberately shied away from getting serious, but he didn't tell her that. 'As a boy I was lost without my mother. I could never understand why such a beautiful, giving person should die so young. There was so much anger and grief trapped inside me sometimes I think I can still never get rid of it. Falling in love is delicious enough. *Loving* is something else again. Losing can be truly ruinous.'

She felt the truth of that. 'I just don't accept you haven't had women in love with you.' Take Lilli Denby, for instance. She also thought of her sister,

Violette. Both of them were definitely looking forward to getting to know more of Linc Mastermann.

'That disturbs you?' he asked, exhilarated to think it might.

'The short answer? What I think about *you* is dangerous.' And *dazzling*.

'Perhaps I feel the same way,' he returned with a short laugh.

'I came home for a holiday.'

'Know what I think, Daniela?' He glanced at her sideways. Her beautiful hair was a halo around her honey-skinned face. 'You came home for some kind of respite. Maybe even to hide away.'

'Carry on, Herr Freud. That's very melodramatic.'

'You're that kind of woman.' He shrugged. 'Wherever you are, you'd be the centre of male attention Some men soak up a woman's beauty like a sponge.'

'You're one of them,' she pointed out.

'I'd be the first to admit it,' he said, silvery green eyes sparkling, clear as crystal.

'Carl, I hardly know you. Surely *some* caution should prevail?'

He looked across at her without a smile. 'I understand your concerns. I share them in a way. But some things, like basic instincts, have a way of cutting through our best intentions. We could act conventionally, take months getting to know one another, but both of us are at a time in our lives when our instincts override caution. We're attracted to one another?'

'Yes.' She turned her head away, but openly acknowledged it. Their attraction had sprung fully formed.

'So, will you have dinner with me and forget your anxieties? I thought we could go to Guy's restaurant and do a little harmless criticising of his chef.'

That brought forth a real smile. 'We'd have our work cut out doing that. Anyway, as I understand it, it's always fully booked on a Saturday evening.'

'Well, very recklessly I booked a table,' he told her nonchalantly. 'It helps to be Guy's good friend. Please say you'll come.' He glanced at her, seeing how her long dark eyelashes were quivering against the golden bloom of her cheek. 'You know you want to.'

She nodded, but her expression was troubled. 'What I'm wondering is what *you* really want?' she said.

He reached out with his left hand and grasped the tips of her fingers.

It was like drowning in a sea of sensuality.

He picked her up at seven on the dot, found her waiting outside the bistro, sitting at one of the *al fresco* tables. Inside it was packed, so tables and chairs had been set strategically outside to accommodate the overflow. When she saw his car she stood up, gathered her little evening bag, said goodnight to the other people at the table, then walked towards him.

She looked a dream, he thought. Her beautiful dark blond hair, swinging free, caught all the light. He could feel ripple upon ripple of desire rush through his body. She wore a shade of green that suited her beautifully—apple-green, he thought. It was strapless, the bodice clinging to her delicate breasts, the skirt short and floaty. His eyes ran from her face down her body to her slender golden legs. She was wearing very high heels. That struck him as incredibly sexy.

'You look wonderful,' he said, taking her hand for a moment and carrying it to his lips. He was oblivious to the effect they were having on the couples at the tables until one guy gave a whistle so expressive it said it all. Devilment in his eyes, Linc returned the wave, before murmuring to Daniela, 'Let's go. It feels a bit like the red carpet out here.' He opened the passenger door for her.

A minute later they pulled away, to a few more appreciative cheers.

'Next time we won't make it so public,' he said dryly.

She smiled. 'We can face that when it comes.'

'You are staying with your family?' He had taken that for granted.

She glanced at his dark dynamic profile. If she had dressed up for him he had returned the compliment—or more probably he always dressed with style. Either way, he looked terrific.

'Actually, I'm renting an apartment while I'm here. There's not really enough room for me with the family, although everyone wanted me to stay. But I wasn't going to crowd them. I'm close by. That's the main thing.'

He was taken by surprise. 'So where's close by? Or is that a big secret?'

'View Point,' she said.

'I know it.'

'I thought you might.'

They drove down an avenue of palms, the headlights flickering over smooth green trunks and garden beds alight with tiny blossomed star jasmine used extensively as ground cover. Smoothly they turned into the car park. Cool with the air-conditioning flowing through the car, it proved much warmer out in the scented night air, redolent of flowers. With one hand barely grazing the smooth skin of her back he led her up the couple of stone steps to the restaurant. They could hear the humming of conversation even before they got inside.

Everything reflected light and glitter—the silver fire of wall mirrors, huge silver chandeliers suspended in the air, appropriately elegant furnishings, luxuriant golden canes in polished brass pots, delicate orchids taking wing in the centre of candle-lit tables, and floor-to-ceiling windows which by day gave a splendid view over the vineyards and by night showed a floodlit terrace, where antique garden carts overflowed with many varieties of colourful flowers, above them a sky full of stars.

The *maître d'*, smartly dressed in navy with a gold trim, greeted them like favoured customers, then led them to a window table.

'I love it here,' Daniela said when they were alone, her high cheekbones warmed with pleasure.

Linc looked around him appreciatively. 'Everything Guy does he does well. He's not only one of the top wool producers in the country, he's a wonderful businessman as well. He has a stake in lots of enterprises.'

'I'd say he'll make a wonderful husband, too,' Daniela smiled, her beautiful mouth tilting upwards.

'Would you give up your career to go off and get married?' he asked, watching her face in the candle glow.

She lifted her eyes to him. Her actual intention was, in time, to direct chefs working under her. 'Couldn't I have both?'

He leaned back in his chair, studying the flawless planes of her face. 'I don't see why not. But it could get difficult when children arrived.'

'Then I guess the career goes on hold for a while.'

'So you *do* want to get married?'

'Of course!' She made a little expressive gesture with her hands. 'What makes you think I wouldn't want to?'

He wanted to bombard her with lots of questions, though he knew he shouldn't. Not now. He wanted her to relax and enjoy herself. For himself, it was almost impossible to unwind. He wanted her as he had never wanted a woman before in his life. Desire at that level could be a tyranny.

'Just checking,' he said, giving her a smile.

The food, when it arrived, not only tasted wonderful, it looked like a work of art. Everything was perfect—the entrée of seafood, the roasted grain-fed lamb carved to perfection over creamed potatoes, with side dishes of perfect little baby vegetables so tender they melted in the mouth.

Daniela wanted to try the green tea crêpes served with mandarin sauce and a dash of orange liqueur.

'I'll have that as well,' Linc told the waiter, handing back the menus. 'Our compliments to the chef. I haven't eaten better.'

'I won't take that as an insult,' Daniela joked a little later.

'Well, you know what I mean.' He shrugged. 'One has to leave the chef feeling happy. Besides, as you told me yourself, I have yet to try your specialties. I can't wait. Great food would cheer anyone up. It'll be a very lucky man who wins your hand, Daniela.'

Later, when they were lingering over coffee, a tall, striking young woman, in an eye-catching cobalt-blue dress, threaded her way rather recklessly through the tables towards them.

Daniela's face must have revealed a shadow of her dismay. She had an idea Violette had had a little too much to drink. The very last thing she needed was some sort of confrontation—such as the Denbys exerting their territorial rights…

'What is it?' Linc asked, turning slightly to follow her gaze. 'Oh-oh—it's Violette.'

Violette, swaying slightly, arrived at their table, smiling over her inner rage, blissfully unaware it was the smile of a tigress. She had spotted their arrival the minute they stood in the foyer, waiting for the *maître d'* to show them to their table. She hadn't been the only one interested. Any number of people—some with knife and fork halfway to their mouths—had broken off to stare politely. There was a trick to doing that. The only thing that had surprised her was that there hadn't been a scattering of applause.

She herself had broken into a sort of sarcastic quip about their entrance—she excelled at that kind of thing—but for once no one had paid attention. It had been bad enough suffering her cousin, Alana, but now there was this exotic Italian creature. For the umpteenth time in her life Violette had felt a flood of jealousy. It was that which had caused her to over-indulge with the wine.

Linc rose to his impressive height at Violette's approach. He was seeing the funny side of it. Lilli in the morning, Violette at night.

'How are you, Violette?' He looked down at her.

For answer, she reached out and cupped one side of his face proprietorially with her hand. 'Exhausted,' she moaned. 'I had a few days in Sydney with friends. They ran me ragged.' She transferred her blue gaze to Daniela. 'Hello, there. We met at the wedding, remember?'

Daniela inclined her head gracefully. 'You and Lilli made beautiful bridesmaids.'

'Would you like to sit down for a moment, Violette?' Linc asked. Violette was reasonably steady on her feet, but one never knew. He looked towards a waiter, who surged forward with an extra chair.

'I must be quick,' Violette said, sinking very

languidly into it. 'No one seems to say *anything* to each other if I'm not there. One of my roles in life is to be the life and soul of the party. Lilli tells me you showed her over your house?' She turned to Linc thinking he looked so at home, with his classy clothes and stunning good looks. She just loved his extraordinary eyes. They were like light-filled peridots in his darkly tanned face.

Linc smiled sardonically. 'I don't think it was to her taste.'

Violette gazed moved momentarily heaven-ward. 'You should have asked *me*. Lilli knows nothing about interior design, renovations—that kind of thing. *I* did a stint with a top-notch design firm some years back. I'd be only too happy to give you a few ideas.' A slow smile accompanied the *double entendre*. 'All it takes is to plan a date.'

'Then I'll let you know,' Linc responded, with a glint in his eyes.

A little more eye-rolling from Violette. This time in Daniela's direction. 'I love your dress. Who is the designer?' Unexpectedly she reached out and fingered the fabric of Daniela's skirt. 'Silk chiffon. It's so *you*!'

'Thank you,' Daniela said.

'It looks very, very expensive, but I suppose it wasn't?' She offered a little commiserating smile.

'Well, it all depends on what you'd call expensive,' Daniela said.

'I shouldn't say this…' Violette lowered her rather haughty voice '…but for me money isn't a problem. Now, I really should go back to my table. They'll be missing me.'

'Why don't I walk you back?' Linc suggested, already on his feet. He had calculated how far Violette might get before lurching into something.

'What a lovely idea!' Violette took his arm and held on as if the two of them were missing at sea. 'I want you to meet my friends. We're bound to be seeing a lot of each other.' She glanced back over her shoulder. 'Nice to see you, Donelda.'

If Violette had been trying to take a rise out of her, it didn't work. Daniela swallowed a laugh. She didn't envy the man caught between Violette and Lilli. And right now that was Linc.

They hardly spoke on the way back to town, their minds and bodies hooked on the powerful physical attraction that was binding them ever tighter. Linc had thought he would be returning her to the safety of the family home, a Mediterranean-style residence with white stucco and terracotta tiles on the outskirts of town. It was an attractive and well-kept house, but pint-sized when compared with what he was used to. He could well understand why Daniela had opted to give her family their space. But now everything had changed. Daniela had her own apartment. Thre was no way he could take her back to the motel, even if she consented to go. He was in no doubt she wouldn't, even if other young women of his acquaintance would have agreed without a second thought.

They turned into South Banksia Street, a fashionable part of town, dominated by the high-rise View Point apartments which he happened to know were expensive. He had looked over them when he had first arrived, but opted to go with the motel, which was situated farther into the valley. He pulled into a parking spot and cut the engine.

'Well, do I see you to your door?' He turned his head to her. He had often heard an expression— hell, he had even used it himself—when friends and acquaintances got caught up in relationships that screamed danger. *God, what gets into people?* He knew now. Desire for this woman had got into him. It was running through his body like flame.

Again a little hand gesture. 'Is that a good idea?'

He sighed, his light eyes burning over her. 'I can't think of a better one right at this moment. I want to make love to you, Daniela, as little or as much as you like.'

There—that was over and done with. You threw down the gauntlet.

She shook her head, almost sadly. 'Would it be all that easy to call a stop?'

He smiled, but there was an edgy down-curve to his mouth. 'I haven't actually had that experience, but I'm damned sure if a woman says no, I'll heed it.'

'And what if I don't wish to say no?' There was a slight break in her voice. 'So far what is between us I can control.'

With her admission he lost all thought. His hand flicked out and he caught her small-boned fingers. The trembling transferred itself to him like a sensual vibration. 'You must be doing a whole lot better than I. I wanted you from the moment I laid eyes on you.'

'And you feel this to be a unique experience?' she asked, as though she could see him tiring of her and moving on.

He laughed harshly. 'I told you once before, Daniela, you could have made it big as a shrink. Anyway, whatever you wish, I intend to see you safely to your door.'

'Very well, then.' She remained where she was until he came around to her side and opened the door.

As it happened no one was in the foyer or

waiting for the lift. They rode it alone, both of them staring straight ahead. They had talked about many things over dinner, a man and a woman accepting each other as equals and enjoying the effortless flow of conversation. He had, in fact, told Daniela a number of things he had thought he had forgotten, perhaps they were better forgotten—and she had really listened. Needless to say he hadn't told her about Cheryl. He wouldn't, even if a suitable occasion arose. Cheryl had been doing her level best to make a nasty mess of all their lives. He knew himself to be blameless of any wrongdoing, but what man was mad enough to trust to the integrity of a scorned woman?

The lift door opened silently. They stepped out into the softly lit, thickly carpeted hallway. Three apartments to this floor. If apartment life suited, the View Point, looking out at the steeply rising blue ranges, was a good place to live.

At her door Daniela looked up at him with brilliant unfathomable eyes. 'I expect you'd like to see inside?'

God, alone! He tried to hold himself steady. How could he define what he was feeling? Love? Infatuation? Intoxication? A driving need to want a woman just for herself? And not just the here and now. It wasn't simple lust. It wasn't complex lust. What he felt was so much more than that. He had *found* her.

Yet when he spoke his voice was smooth, almost nonchalant. 'I'd like to know what sort of a home you've made for yourself.'

'Then please come in.'

Both of them were fighting hard to keep up their guard. Daniela was thinking herself on the point of disintegration. She ached for him to make love to her. Yet here in the quiet corridor, self-control reigned.

It gave way immediately once they were inside, the door shut tight against the outside world.

Daniela was standing small and slender, her back to him, her body as poised and alert as a dancer's, blazingly aware of what was to happen next.

Linc, too, felt that taut leap of fire. Of their own accord his hands found her bare shoulders, shaping them, gently exploring the delicate bones. She didn't move. He could smell her perfume, haunting but not pervasive, and beneath that the exquisite essence of *her*. He had made her a promise and he meant it, but he felt the danger-ous frailty of his self-control. It was a wonder she couldn't hear his heavy heartbeats. Slowly, irre-sistibly, he lowered his head, letting his mouth and the tip of his tongue trail down beneath her ear to the silky column of her throat. The taste of her! She moved slightly, but it was back into him, her blond head falling against his shoulder. Now his arms moved to wrap her, to bind her to him. In a way the action betrayed him—because there was so much to betray.

The pressure grew. The tempo picked up.

When he turned her to him Daniela was so overwhelmed she didn't murmur or whisper one word of protest. Instead she let him kiss her with all the burning slowness he desired, until it became too much for her and she felt herself surrender completely.

'If you're going to stop me, it has to be *now*.' His strong, muscular arms were trembling. Even his voice sounded different—younger, shaken, husky in his throat. All the emotion locked up within him come to the boil. He was desperate to be a part of her, to make her a part of him. His hands had moved down over her small perfect breasts, full of passionate yearning. He had never felt like this before. The silk seemed to evaporate beneath his touch.

Her answer, when it came, was a soft, fluttery whisper. Like him, she sounded dazed. Her arms came up to encircle his neck. 'It's all right, Carl. I want you.'

The world spun.

He didn't speak, but picked her up.

* * *

It was almost three in the morning before Linc pulled into the motel, parking his car quietly, then letting himself into his room. He stood in the dark for long moments. Even the darkness seemed transformed. Without turning on the lights, he stripped off his clothes, laying them on a chair. His body ached for her even though they had made love until they were spent on splendour.

He knew every inch of her, nothing hidden. So tumultuous had been their hunger they had made love under bright lights, the bed a cool white field of cotton, scarcely aware of the illumination spilling over them because they couldn't stop or let go. Whatever he'd wanted, she had risen to meet him, the two of them physically, wondrously compatible. He had never known such intimacy existed. It had left him feeling exultant and a little unstrung. He sensed it was the same for her. It was almost as though for a few short hours they had forgotten everyone and everything—even their own identities. He hadn't wanted to get up and leave her. He just wanted to be with her for a thousand years.

You and me.

Always.

Or was that just a dream?

CHAPTER SIX

ALTHOUGH inside Cheryl Mastermann was screaming with boredom and frustration, she kept to her routine. Ben adored her, but she couldn't do a single thing out of the ordinary. She wouldn't have been a bit surprised to learn he kept tabs on her.

Most people in the district regarded her as the trophy wife—the *third* Mrs Ben Mastermann. She knew she wasn't liked. There had only ever been the one Mrs Mastermann so far as the district was concerned, and that had been the late Barbara. Wife Number Two—Valerie, socially well placed—hadn't gone the distance but had been reasonably well liked. In no way was she, Cheryl, an acceptable replacement for either—especially Barbara, the mother of Ben's two splendid sons. Barbara's premature death was universally regarded as a tragedy.

Cheryl had met him at a fundraiser on the Queensland Gold Coast, a holiday destination for anyone seeking the sun, the surf, the casino, and a frenzied night-life if you wanted it. As soon as she'd found out Ben Mastermann was loaded she had always managed to squeeze herself into the chair beside him. It hadn't been as easy as she'd thought to get him to sleep with her—most guys took advantage of that right off—but when she had, flattering him immensely, she'd had the multimillionaire all stitched up. Anyway, Ben was a fine-looking man—and plenty virile enough, as it turned out.

All might have gone along smoothly enough, only next she'd met his two sons. Chuck was a nice guy. No problem. She'd liked him right off. The other one, Linc, who really hadn't wanted to meet her—she understood from Ben he had been a mommy's boy—had shaken her to her very foundations. He looked dangerous—kind of *wild*. Nobody's idea of a mommy's boy, although it was certain he had loved his mother and continued to mourn her. Both brothers were tall, dark and handsome, but Linc made Chuck look dead ordinary. She would never forget the *lash* of his eyes—silvery green, sultry, brooding. It brought out her masochistic streak. So, instead of falling in love with the father—her husband—she had fallen violently in love with his younger son, when she hadn't believe she would ever genuinely fall in love with *anyone*. She was thirty-two years old—though she looked nothing like it—and it was no secret she'd played the field. When she was twenty she had even almost got married. Instead she had jilted Dean at the altar. Turned out she hadn't been pregnant after all. What a lucky break!

Though she had tried every way she knew how to find out where Linc had gone, all lips were sealed for her, and Ben refused point-blank to speak about his younger son, dubbing him 'a traitor'. Even she, who had no interest whatsoever in Gilgarra as a working station, knew as well as anybody that Linc was the driving force behind the whole operation. Chuck was just fine in the second chair, but everyone on the station was feeling Linc's absence. But she knew why Linc had had to leave, even if he had never spoken a word. He was secretly as nuts about her as she was about him.

Her mind had already begun the leap towards leaving Ben—though she wasn't such a fool she didn't recognise the danger. Ben was a proud man, and he regularly flew off the handle. Not with her—he wasn't that sort of man—but everyone knew Ben was furious with Linc for his defection. So where had Linc skedaddled to? No one disappeared into thin air. She could find out if she put her mind to it, but she had the dismal notion Ben might find out what she was doing, too. And, hell, if she got on the wrong side of him he might kick her out before she was ready. Ben was capable of anything. He had got her to sign a pre-nup agreement, which didn't say a lot about his trust in her.

There were a lot of things that frightened a girl. One was being left on her own. The other was being left broke.

Today she was on her way to a luncheon in town—another fundraiser for the local hospital. Whatever people secretly thought of her and said behind her back, as Ben Mastermann's wife, they were careful to include her on the important committees. Most committee women were older than she, and she knew they were green with jealousy over her youth and good looks. As always, she was done up to the nines. She wanted Ben to be proud of her even if she daydreamed of cleaning out his bank accounts and taking off to the South of France with Linc. She was struck by an image of him and groaned aloud.

It was as she was approaching Ben's study, her footsteps muffled by the long Persian runner, that she heard Chuck say, 'I don't need this, Dad. I work my butt off, you know that, but I'm not Linc.'

'Goddamned right, you're not. You're loyal. Your brother left us in the lurch. What the hell is he up to?'

'I thought you didn't want to know?'

'Son, I only have to lift my hand to the phone,' Ben growled. 'Where is he? Where did he go? What are his plans? His mother and his grandfather left him money.'

'And he has a half-share in Gilgarra, Dad, after you've gone.'

'After I'm gone?' Ben bellowed. 'I'm not planning on going anywhere real soon. For all you know Cheryl could bear me another son. We're working on it. If I had my way Linc would be cut out of everything. He doesn't deserve it.'

'Yes, he does,' Chuck answered flatly. 'You never tried at all with Linc, did you? You always favoured me.'

'On the other hand your mother favoured Linc over both of us,' Ben returned bitterly.

'It wasn't like that!' Chuck protested. 'Mum loved us all. But you didn't want to share her with anyone—even your own sons. Linc was right to go away. I shouldn't be telling you this, but he's bought a place of his own. And knowing Linc it won't take him long to make a name for himself in the industry.'

A moment of deadly quiet, then Ben snapped out, 'You mean he's been able to acquire a halfway decent property? Do I have to drag it out of you an inch at a time, boy? Where the hell is he?'

'All right, Dad, calm down,' Chuck begged swiftly. 'This flying into a rage can't be good for you. Just between the two of us, Linc has bought a place called Briar's Ridge. It's in a valley beyond the Hunter. The owner, a man called Alan Callaghan, died some time last year. Linc's friend Guy Radcliffe put in a word for him.'

'Radcliffe!' Ben let out another bellow. 'Ah, the rich, powerful Radcliffes—old family, old money. I just bet Guy was a big help. Probably came in as a backer.'

'No, Linc went in alone. I'd be grateful if you didn't tell Cheryl.'

'And why in the hell would I do that?' Ben yelled. 'Better yet, why would Cheryl want to know? She never said anything to me, and I never saw anything first hand, but Linc never did a damned thing to make her feel welcome in her own home. He resented her on account of your mother. I *never* discuss Linc with Cheryl. It's been mighty peaceful around here without him.'

'Then why are you missing him, Dad?' Chuck asked quietly, having the last word.

Cheryl backed up very quickly, her heart in her throat. Chuck could come out of the study at any time. She didn't want him to catch her eavesdropping as though her life depended on it. Little tears gathered in her eyes. Her prayers had been answered. Now she knew where Linc was. At the end of the month Ben and a group of wool producers had a trip to China lined up. As far as she knew he was expecting her to go with him. She would have to come up with a good excuse to stay home.

As Chuck strode into the entrance hall, on his way back to work, Cheryl appeared to be just coming down the stairs. 'Hi there, Chuck,' she called, giving him a bright, friendly smile. 'Man in a hurry?'

He nodded pleasantly enough. 'On your way out? You look great.' Even so, Chuck considered that in marrying Cheryl his father had made a horrendous mistake.

'Why, thank you!' Cheryl trilled. 'Your dad in the study? He always likes to see me dressed up.'

And *undressed*, Chuck thought bitterly, his nerves badly frayed. He had told Linc he wouldn't tell anybody. Now this! At least Cheryl wouldn't know. Chuck was sure his father would keep that piece of information to himself—and thank God for that! He had the dismal notion that beneath the fluff Cheryl was a nasty piece of work.

In the weeks that followed Linc had the sense of living on a different plane. Whatever he was doing—and he was extremely busy—there simply weren't enough hours in the day, what with furnishing the house, stocking the property, putting on another man, meeting up with his fellow breeders, acquiring and training a pair of truly excellent, tireless sheep dogs. But Daniela kept insinuating herself into his mind. When he was with her all was right with the world. It was when he was away from her the feeling was especially strong—and that was most of the time, because she, too, was kept busy.

He was beginning to think he was falling for her, though he never let that out. Neither, for that matter, did *she* put words to her deepest feelings.

There had been no natural progression. Their passion had all the power and danger of driving his sports car at high speed, that was how big and fast it was. Their affair was virtually free of admissions, as though admissions carried a high degree of risk, and he sometimes felt the two of them were suspended in time. If their relationship continued they would reach a point where it wouldn't be safe *not* to face what was in them.

He wondered if her family—her mother, surely—knew the strength of their connection. Probably. Mothers had an infallible sense of such things. Though it was not as if he saw Daniela more than once or twice a week. Both of them, it seemed, were better than most people at hiding their true feelings, yet inside he felt as though a dam had burst, flooding his entire body with emotion. If she went away, went back to London, he wasn't sure how he would react. She had become the focus of his world. All he wanted, *needed* now, was to be near her.

Did he want her too much?

Was it possible to want a woman too much? All he knew was he couldn't take in the full extent of his hunger. He hadn't been prepared for it, for things happening over which a man had no control. He couldn't even control his hands when he was with her, holding her, kissing her, loving her. Even days after they made love he still felt the aftershocks.

Was it the same for her? He wanted to confront her with it. At the same time he knew confrontation at this stage of their love affair was potentially a danger. He was sure something had happened to Daniela in London. Something she wasn't comfortable with but wasn't about to confide. Maybe he had to talk first. Get Cheryl off his chest. He wouldn't put it past Cheryl to pop up out of the blue. Some women could twist anything around in their heads. Fantasise. Cheryl had acted as if they had shared an illicit passion. Maybe she truly believed it? Maybe she had reasoned the way he had shunned her only hid a fatal attraction? God knew what went on inside that airhead. All he knew was he didn't relish the idea of confronting his volatile dad, pointing a rifle at him. His dad was an 'act first and talk later' kind of guy…

Daniela was surprised when Violette and Lilli Denby made a reservation for lunch at the bistro.

'You're becoming famous, *cara mia*,' her grandfather told her. 'The word has gone out.'

Both sisters gave every appearance of enjoying the lightest lunch on the menu—scallops with watercress and a Vietnamese dressing, no entrée, no dessert—and they shared a chilled bottle of Cabernet Sauvignon. It was afterwards they got down to business, with Violette predictably taking the lead. Daniela privately thought Lilli would have developed better without Violette for a big sister. At least Rose had fought free.

Violette had requested a word, so Daniela finished off what she was doing, gave some instructions to her very capable mother, whipped off her big white apron and went out front. The bistro was slowly emptying, and as she threaded her way through to the Denby sisters' table she was repeatedly stopped by customers who wanted her to know how much they had enjoyed the whole experience of coming to the bistro. It might well be that the family would have to shift to bigger premises some time soon. Since she had been home she had passed on a lot of her expertise, and it showed. She had a dream of one day opening her own restaurant. She might employ her family—they worked closely and well together—but she had progressed much too far to settle for bistro dining.

As she approached the Denby table she had the sensation of two pairs of blue eyes burning over her, of blond heads inclined conspiratorially towards each other. As ever, both sisters were beautifully dressed, perhaps a touch overdressed, with not a gleaming hair out of place. She, on the other hand, had been working more or less flat out for hours, and could feel the heat of the kitchen in her cheeks.

Violette gave her a big smile, showing her perfect teeth, but her tone was brittle. 'Please sit down.' She gave a laugh.

Whatever did that laugh mean? Daniela reached for a chair at the adjoining table, now empty, turned it, then sat down. 'How can I help you?' she asked pleasantly, but didn't pick up on any wave of friendliness from the sisters. Rather, they—and Violette in particular—appeared to be playing some sort of power game. Was it possible they were going to ask her to leave town? Such was their arrogance she wouldn't put it past them. The thought calmed and amused her.

'Great lunch, by the way,' Lilli told her with a note of surprise.

'I'm glad.' Daniela inclined her head. 'I do hope you'll come again, and perhaps bring your friends?'

'We'd love to,' Violette said. 'The thing is we're more or less committed to Guy's restaurant. Multi-award-winning, as I expect you know. But for a light lunch here is fine.'

'Is that what you wanted to tell me?' Daniela asked, her pleasant tone slipping a little.

Lilli responded swiftly, a little colour in her cheeks. 'No…well, yes… Tell her, Vi.'

Violette gave her sister an arctic smile. '*Violette*, dear.'

Lilli's trained answer was immediate. '*Violette*.'

'I'd be grateful if you would,' Daniela said, her calm returned. 'I still have some things to finish off.'

'Of course!' Violette sat back as if to say, *What do you have to do? What does it really matter?* 'I'm planning a dinner party for a few friends at the end of the month, on a Saturday night,' she said, as though announcing a meeting of the Commonwealth Heads of State. 'Just twenty of us in all—a small party. We'd like you to handle it. It would be a smart business move for you. If it goes well I'm sure you'll get plenty of spin-offs.'

So no written invitation, then? Business, not

pleasure. 'Who do you usually use?' Daniela asked. Saturday was her night with Carl. She longed for Saturday every single day of the week.

Violette shrugged, her blue eyes shiny. 'Oh, one of the chefs from Guy's restaurant. This time we thought we'd try you. The talk around the town is you're a marvellous cook.'

'I am,' Daniela said simply, no false modesty.

Violette laughed, as if success had gone to Daniela's head, but Lilli spoke up. 'Oh, please tell us you're interested,' she said. 'We'd want to see the menu, of course. Stuff like that.'

'And there's no need for budgeting,' said Violette, a woman who was only used to the finer things in life. 'Buy the best.'

'I always do,' Daniela said, giving a slight frown. 'I don't know, Violette…' She had an idea Violette could be just cruel enough to want to see her make a mess of things. Then again she might be overreacting. Violette would hardly wish to spoil her own dinner party.

'How can you knock me back?' Violette opened her eyes wide in amazement. 'What do you normally charge? Whatever it is, I'm prepared to go higher.'

Daniela immediately named a figure she was certain would put the Denby sisters off.

Lilli stared fixedly at the white tablecloth as if

at an invoice. Violette was up for the challenge.
'Then we can rely on you?'

Well, she had no one to blame but herself.
'Certainly,' Daniela said in a businesslike voice.
'I'll prepare two menus, not interchangeable.
Each dish on the set menu will complement the
next. The final say is, of course, yours. The dinner
party will be at your home?'

Violette nodded, her manner suggesting the
guests would be royalty.

'I usually prepare the table,' Daniela said. The
most gracious and aristocratic lady of her acquaintance had allowed her to do that—indeed, encour-
aged her. 'I choose the linen, bone china,
silverware, crystal, flowers. All to complement the
food. I imagine you have plenty to choose from?'

'Exquisite things!' Violette confirmed with her
usual haughtiness, trying unsuccessfully to hide
her shock. Who was this little upstart to take over
the table setting and the flowers when *she* excelled
at that sort of thing? But those great brooding
dark eyes were on her, probing her motives. 'We'll
leave it entirely up to you,' she said.

The truth was, Violette's great hope was that
Daniela Adami would make a real mess of things.
It might teach her a well-deserved lesson. Ms
Adami had to learn she was way out of her class,
and the sooner the better. If she thought for a

moment she could snare Linc Mastermann then she was out of her tiny mind.

Daniela drove out of the canopy of trees and into the broad driveway. He was waiting for her up on the verandah, but as she slid into a parking spot in the shade he walked down the short flight of steps to join her.

'So what brings you here on a weekday afternoon?' Linc called, as if he hadn't seen her for weeks instead of a few days, his body and even his soul stirring. 'I thought you'd be working?'

'Forgive my weakness.' She smiled up at him, thrilled by his welcome, removing her sunglasses. She was wearing a summery white dress that showed off her flawless skin.

He gave in to his feelings. He pulled her to him, one-armed, and kissed her gently, then harder, tasting the peaches of her mouth. Or was it apricots? It was a marvellous feeling to have her here. Marvellous to kiss her in the blazing sunlight. It had been a magnificent day. Late afternoon was still hot.

'I'll forgive you anything,' he muttered. 'Just so long as it brings you to me.'

'Well, it has.' She lingered in his arms. 'I must be feeling perilous.'

'More perilous than usual?' He slipped an arm around her, leading her to the house.

'Let's forget I said that.' She had only just arrived, yet she was feeling the sizzle of excitement. At the same time she felt she belonged there. With him. It was a glorious feeling, yet in some ways it scared her.

'How long can you stay?' He looked down on her shining hair. It made a wonderful contrast with her dark eyes and golden skin.

'As long as you like. But I don't want to take you from your work. You've been quite a hit in the valley. Everyone seems enormously impressed.' Especially the female population. He would turn any woman's head.

'Oh, yes? Who told you this?'

He didn't sound in the least concerned. 'The word has gone around,' she said. 'People talk. You know that. It's a big valley with a small population. You've been the focus of all the attention of late. The Sextons come into the bistro at least once a week. They're very pleasant people. Tom thinks you're going to make your mark in the valley, and he and Grace already consider you a good neighbour. I don't know, but Tom said he once knew or knows of your father.'

'That would be "knows of",' Linc said, with a sinking feeling, though it was no surprise that anyone in the pastoral world would know of the Mastermanns of Gilgarra. How the hell had he thought he was going to keep anything secret? If Chuck didn't spill it out in an unguarded moment, the news of his buying Briar's Ridge would inevitably leak back to his father.

And the ticking time bomb—Cheryl.

He would have to deal with that when it happened.

Inside the homestead, she turned to him with a gasp of pure pleasure. 'Good heavens, Carl! You've done wonders since I was last here.'

He was gratified by her expression. 'I wanted to surprise you. Chuck sent a lot of my stuff on.'

'I can see that.' She loved the Southeast Asian influence, a collection of artefacts, stone sculptures, tables, chairs and chests. The art on the walls was bold, modern, calling for one's own interpretation. 'You must be working twenty-four-seven,' she said, turning to look at him with unconcealed admiration. If he were, he was fairly blazing with energy.

'I've never had the opportunity of doing my own thing,' he said with satisfaction. 'Your coming into Sydney with me made a big difference. Because we were able to settle on most of the furniture there and then, I was happy to let the removalists put it all in place. Of course, I had to shift a few things around, but that was fun. I haven't touched the kitchen. It works at the moment. Like a cup of coffee? I bought the beans at the bistro, so they'll be good.'

'A cold drink would be even better,' she said, walking towards a seated gilt Buddha. It sat on top of a carved chest, flanked by two extraordinary silver lamps balancing on three legs.

'Sri Lankan,' he told her. 'They were originally altar lamps. Do you know what Sri Lanka means?'

'Beautiful island, isn't it?'

'Right in one. Guy and I stayed with family friends there. Both their sons were sent to our school and later on to uni. The family used to own a huge rubber plantation in the days when Sri Lanka was Ceylon. Now they have a tea plantation. They're an English-Australian family, but they'll never leave. They really love the place, and I have to say it's very beautiful. The chest with the Buddha on it comes from there, as do the ebony chairs. I like a mix.'

'Especially when it works as well as this.' She turned about. 'Did you paint that wall saffron?' It was spectacular against all the white.

'I did. It was well after midnight before I finished. The colour really sets off the big painting, don't you think?'

She nodded, studying the huge painting that might have been an abstract tapestry. 'All those blues!' She was forever seeing him in a new light.

'The bed arrived, by the way. Ready to deal with that?' His silvery green eyes glittered over her.

'Only if I want to forget the rest of the world for a few hours,' she said, a telling warmth rising to her cheeks.

'And don't you?'

'You're too good a lover, Carl,' she said, excitement flooding in on her.

'And you're a dream to make love to.'

She didn't betray what that admission did to her beyond the trembling in her hands.

Slowly she followed him into the kitchen, loving his lean, elegant frame, the width of his shoulder. His shirts and jackets always sat so beautifully. 'Violette and Lilli called in for lunch today,' she told him in a conversational voice.

'What a surprise!' His tone was ultra-dry. He bent to the refrigerator, withdrew two bottles of Coke. 'This okay?' He turned back to her, his skin giving off a wonderful bronze glow.

'Fine.' She really didn't care, as long as it was cold. 'They gave me quite a shock.'

'And more to come?' He hunted up one of the best glasses for her, intending to drink his from the bottle.

'As a matter of fact, yes. They've asked me to cater a dinner party Violette is giving a few Saturdays from now. I didn't want to, so I made my asking price outrageously high, but it all rebounded on me, I'm afraid. Violette agreed. I'm not sure why exactly. Lilli kept her eyes glued to the tablecloth.'

'Probably as shocked as you were,' he said wryly.

'I think she knew better than to intervene. Violette is, without question, the boss.'

'She'll make a hell of a wife!' he said, pouring her Coke and placing it before her.

'Does that mean splendid, or what?'

'What do you think?' he asked with a rakish smile. 'The Denby sisters are very attractive to look at. One might ask the question why they're not married?'

She took a long sip of her cold drink. 'Well, Violette did carry the torch for Guy. She's since dropped it for *you*. The pity of it is, I think Lilli has the wild idea in her head that she can outmanoeuvre her big sister.'

'Should I be worried?' His tongue curled over his beautifully cut upper lip, tasting Coke.

'I think so. I'm betting Violette sends you a written invitation—or maybe she'll deliver it in person.'

He thrust back the unruly lock of hair that insisted on springing forward onto his forehead. 'She already has.' He waited for her reaction.

'She's a fast worker.' Daniela clasped her frosty

glass to her. He hated that errant lock. She loved it. 'No doubt you accepted?'

He moved nearer her. 'There was a problem,' he said. 'As far as I'm concerned Saturday night means *you*. I'd back off dinner with every other woman alive for you.'

'But you accepted Violette's invitation?' She was surprised how cool and collected she sounded.

He didn't say anything but continued moving towards her, blocking the sunlight streaming through the windows, blocking her entire vision of the world. Though it thrilled her, she didn't really know how to deal with it. Gently he placed his hands on her shoulders. The fingertips were callused from hard work, but she didn't mind that in the least. It only served to make his hands on her soft skin even more erotic. 'The thing is,' he said, looking down at her wryly, 'the party is for *me*.'

'*Wh-a-t?*' Shock and a lick of anger shook her voice. Instantly she regretted it. What they had, no matter how deep and elemental, wasn't any sort of a commitment. Neither of them, even in the throes of passion, had cried out the dreaded L word.

He curled a hand around her nape, beneath the thick silky bell of her hair. 'It's supposed to be a "welcome to the valley" sort of thing. A "neigh-bourly thing" was how Violette described it. She and Lilli want me to meet their friends.'

'So you couldn't possibly refuse?'

'Daniela,' he said gently, 'that would have been very churlish. I know you understand that. I never even asked her if you would be invited—'

'Me?' She shook herself free. 'I could hardly be classed as a friend. Alana made things smooth for me. Easy. But Violette and her sister are out to make things very difficult indeed. One doesn't need an instinctive mind to sense that.'

'Okay, they're jealous,' he agreed. 'Can you blame them? They fear you. You're a beautiful woman. Not only that, you've cut out a career for yourself working with the world's elite chefs in what must be a male-dominated world. You have talent, strength and ambition. Violette and Lilli have been near ruined by their money.'

'And I pity them.' She knew she shouldn't give in to her anger and her deep sense of hurt—it *would* have been very difficult for him to refuse, a newcomer to the valley, dependent on valley goodwill—but she knew she was failing to do so. Restraint had always been her way. Now that restraint was crumbling beyond repair. 'The real question is *why* did they ask me to do the catering?'

'The answer is simple. You're the hot new chef in town. You have winning credentials. In fact, you've made so much of an impression I hear one has to book well in advance to get into the bistro.

All *we* need to do is move Saturday to Sunday. There's a big plus going here. You'll be in a position to showcase your culinary skills to people who do a lot of entertaining.'

'You mean the old families?' she asked, with a tinge of sarcasm.

'I suppose. Anyway, *I'll* be proud of you.'

She turned away quickly. 'Violette didn't mention to you she was going to ask me to do the catering?'

'I would have told you right off.'

'Really?' She turned back, her great dark eyes flashing.

'So, tell me—you don't trust me?'

The question, the sombre way it was put, took her by surprise. 'I'm sorry. I apologize.'

'Yet irrationally some part of you thinks I've failed you?'

She recognised the truth of it. 'We have no commitment, Carl.'

Looking at her, hearing what she said, brought out the weakness in his defences. He threw out an arm beyond him and gathered her in. 'That's funny? No commitment?'

She saw the hard edge to his handsome features. She dropped her eyes.

'Look at me, Daniela,' he ordered. 'I want you so much it scares me, and I know every inch of your beautiful body, but you won't let me get close to you. Something happened to you when you were in London. I want to know but I'm afraid to push it. I don't even know if you intend to go back there.'

'It's personal,' she said, her own weakness causing her to rest against him, her arms of their own accord going around his waist.

'Important?' He ignored the pain in her voice. 'I assume it's some guy?'

She sought his eyes. 'Carl, I wish I could talk about it, but I can't. I want to put the whole thing out of my mind.'

'So you were in love with him?' he asked, very quietly. How could she still be in love with some guy in London and be as she was with *him*?

'No.' Violently she shook her head. 'He was— is—a bit unstable.'

'You mean crazy?' he replied, his tone perplexed and a little bitter. He didn't believe her.

'No, not that at all. I can only explain it as an obsessive nature.' She grew cold at the thought of it.

'Is that so unusual?' he retorted. 'Most men would turn obsessive over *you*. So you had a passionate affair that didn't work out?'

She withdrew her arms, but he didn't let her go. 'No affair,' she said tightly. 'You don't get it. And I don't want to talk about it.'

Abruptly he relented. 'Daniela, if you're frightened of someone, frightened this man will follow you here, I promise you I'll take good care of you. No one will ever hurt you while I'm around.'

She searched his face, knowing he had a very protective attitude towards women. No doubt his great love for his mother was a big factor in that. She knew he was tough. She knew he was strong. She knew he would be ruthless if he had to be. She thought, all things being equal, Gerald Templeton wouldn't have a chance against him. It all came down to whether Gerald had forgotten her or not.

Or perhaps nothing would stop him? In his own way he tortured her.

She leaned her head back against Carl's chest and closed her eyes. Gerald, for all his threatening behaviour, had never had such power over her.

'Come upstairs,' he murmured very quietly into her scented, silky hair. 'I can't be alone with you without wanting to make love to you, Daniela.'

Later, she couldn't even remember walking back through the silent house and up the stairs with him. All was fluid motion and miraculous excitement. She remembered it was he who threw himself down on the splendid carved bed that looked as if it could easily accommodate three or four people. He who lifted his arms to her as she stepped closer, her breath coming fast over her wildly beating heart.

'Come here to me,' he said, his shimmering eyes a mix of hunger, tenderness and an odd compassion.

She leaned over him and kissed him, holding nothing back, one hand flat against his lean cheek, her blond hair falling forward around her face.

He pulled her onto the bed, as easily and as gently as if she were a piece of porcelain.

This was their escape route to ecstasy.

CHAPTER SEVEN

WHAT really got under Gerald's skin was the fact none of Daniela's colleagues—indeed no one who had ever worked with her—would level with him about where she had gone. That rankled badly, although he took good care not to show it. He kept his enquiries to the seemingly casual. A few of the people close to her might have known they had been seeing quite a bit of each other, though he had never been able to get her into his bed. They were taking care to keep what conversation there was to the usual pleasantries. The fellow who worked with her when she did her party catering, Peter, told him in confidence he was pretty sure she had gone back to Italy.

'Danni told me once she ached for Italy. I expect that's where she headed. We all expect a postcard from Rome sooner or later.'

If she had gone to Rome it had proved surprisingly difficult to track her down. But Gerald was not to know he had been deliberately led astray. What Daniela had actually confided to Peter was that she ached for *Australia*.

Templeton's own crowd, the top-notch people, had no idea where she'd gone, couldn't care less although quite a few said it was a pity she had gone because she really was a terrific chef. Oddly enough, Gerald had objected very strongly to her working in kitchens. Such busy, noisy places—all hands working at a frantic pace. Why ever had she chosen such a career? His views on the matter he'd decided to keep to himself—at least for a time. She was maddeningly beautiful and fine company. She even spoke well, with a faint and intriguing Italian accent, but he had never for a moment thought of her as suitable to be his wife. His mother, a woman to be reckoned with, had the right girl in mind—Lady Laurella Marks. He would go along with that. Laurella was a good sort, with a cool, down-to-earth streak and no consuming libido—which was a relief. He could find passion elsewhere. Laurella had missed out a bit in the looks department, but she had dignity and elegance and she could be relied upon to keep a stiff upper lip. Best of all, she had money of her own. And there was, of course, the family name. What he had in mind for Daniela was the role of mistress. He thought in time she would come round to it. She was a working girl, after all. One he rather suspected—or all her beauty—had come from humble roots. Society these days sanctioned mistresses, especially those as beautiful as Daniela.

Imagine his shock—he still hadn't recovered—when she had told him she found his suggestions not only highly objectionable but nauseating.

'And I thought you were a gentleman!'

'I am—and I can do better than that. I'm a real catch.'

'For some women, I suppose. Not for me.'

It was a few weeks after that when he had begun to stalk her. No use hiding it. His fascination with her had turned him into a different man. Either that or it had brought out the worst in him. He phoned her. He e-mailed her, keeping the messages ambiguous. He waited for her wherever she went. Once, she had approached him and told him she would go to the police.

'My dear Daniela, sadly no one will listen to you. I'll have a different story to tell. People know me. They know my family. What are you, after all?'

And now, though it was the last thing he had intended, he had driven her out of London. Obviously she had made a run for it. But sooner or later he would find her. When he least expected it would be the time he would get a break…

It was on a flight home from Zurich that he

found himself seated beside Malcolm McIver, an acquaintance, big in advertising. They talked easily enough most of the flight back, though they would never make friends. It wasn't until they were told to fasten their seatbelts for the landing that McIver turned to him and asked, 'Whatever happened to that gorgeous little Italian girl you used to have on your arm?'

'Oh, that was just to annoy Laurella.' He shrugged it off, man to man.

'Lady Laurella Marks, you mean?' McIver looked at him rather hard.

'Of course. Just a matter of time before we walk down the aisle.'

McIver's expression hardened. 'Wouldn't having an affair with another woman give you a bad name and upset Laurella dreadfully? No wonder—Daniela, wasn't it?—headed off for Australia. I never thought she'd stay with you anyway. Too good, in my opinion.'

Gerald decided to keep that insult very much in mind. If ever he got the opportunity to hurt McIver in business he wouldn't hesitate to sink the boot in. Yet shouldn't he be thanking the man? He had never thought about Australia. To his mind Australia was an absolute backwater. It was *huge*, he knew that, but hardly packed with people.

His eyes lit up with a malevolent gleam. He would find her. As the saying went, persistence would win the day.

Daniela surveyed the Denby formal dining room with satisfaction. She had gone to a lot of trouble and it had paid off. The table looked spectacularly well. It helped that the room was beautiful and spacious, of perfect dimensions, with a lovely high ceiling, moulded and delicately coloured in a design of various fruits. A magnificent antique chandelier hung over the centre of the long table which, when fully extended, could comfortably seat twenty guests and certainly a few more.

With so much to choose from she hadn't had the slightest difficulty deciding on the right napery, the bone china, the silver, the crystal. The Denbys were collectors, and over the long years they had collected many fine things. In every drawer, cupboard and cabinet she had found silver, silverware and a dozen fine bone china dinner sets: Aynsley, Royal Doulton, Wedgwood, Coalport, Mikasa. Deep drawers contained a wealth of fine table linen, including some beautiful Irish linens, both single and double damask, in white and cream.

She felt relief that Mr and Mrs Denby would not be present. They were staying at their Sydney

Harbourside apartment, where they would remain for at least a week.

Gary, her number two at Aldo's, had helped her with the placement of the settings, commenting on the exquisite gold-rimmed crystal wine glasses, three at each setting. Gary and Jules, a determined and remarkably capable seventeen-year-old apprentice Aldo's Bistro had taken on, would be on hand to help her.

The Denby kitchen was the workplace of a serious cook. It was huge, ultra-modern, and fitted with every conceivable appliance, a cooking island, and loads of bench space.

It had been Daniela's idea to use a beautiful almost life-size silver swan that had been stored away at the back of a cabinet as a centrepiece. One of the Denby maids had polished it to perfection, and now it gleamed, its hollow back filled with a profusion of delicate ferns and lovely white orchids with cerise throats. The right flowers were very important—no heavy scent, a full arrangement, but low so the dinner guests could easily see one another across the table. Eight matching silver candlesticks, four to each side of the swan, were spaced down the table. She had deliberated over beautiful lace-trimmed placemats versus a near floor-length Irish linen cloth, a chrysanthemum double damask she fell in love with, and in the end went for that. For a touch of colour she had wound tiny Thai orchids of an incredible shade of purple-blue with trails of gypsophila around the base of the candlesticks. It was a nice touch. The table needed a little colour, and the deep blue was picked up in the rim of the beautiful white bone china.

At first Violette, slowly orbiting the table, wanted to find something glaringly wrong. The fact that it was all so *perfect* gave her quite a jolt. That silver swan had been stuck at the back of a cabinet for years on end, although she seemed to remember her grandmother using it a lot for her flower arrangements. Never on the dining table, however. The arrangements had always graced the library table in the entrance hall as far as she could remember.

Of course Lilli couldn't be counted on to stay aloof. She had gone up to the outsider and taken her hand, swinging it gently.

'It's *wonderful*, Daniela. You're a true artist.'

Violette wanted to silence her with a good hard slap, like when they were kids. Instead she pursed her lips. 'I think I would have preferred table mats—and those little orchids could be a touch too vibrant…' She dragged one a little higher.

Daniela shook her head, thinking she would have to fix it back. 'I don't think so, Violette. So much white needs enlivening.'

Lilli tapped her taller sister playfully on the shoulder. 'Come on, Vi. This is really beautiful. Even Mum hasn't done better.'

Violette glanced at her sister, her finely chiselled nose wrinkling ever so slightly. 'Excuse me, Lilli,' she drawled, 'Mother is famous for her exquisite table settings and her roses. I expected *you* to use roses, Daniela.' She sounded disappointed at Daniela's choice.

'Roses would have been lovely,' Daniela conceded, keeping her sighs to herself. 'But this is a little different, don't you think?'

For her answer Violette made a 'tsk' noise and reached forward to minutely adjust a finely penned placecard. 'I have an infallible eye,' she explained. 'That didn't sit straight.'

Lilli chortled. 'You've just *got* to change something, Vi.'

'God, Lilli—how many times do I have to tell you it's *Violette*. I detest Vi.'

'I wouldn't worry if you called me Lil,' Lilli retorted.

'Why don't we just concentrate on the table?' Violette said. 'Now, let's see. Maybe we should move Zoe a little farther down. There is a pecking order, after all.' She switched a card that said Selina Morris for one that said Zoe Baker. I'm at the head of the table, of course.'

Another eye-roll from Lilli. 'Of *course*!'

'Linc, as guest of honour, is to my right. Did I tell you Linc Mastermann will be coming, Daniela?' Violette said, with a happy flourish.

'You must have. Daniela wrote up the place-cards,' Lilli reminded her, winking at Daniela.

Daniela thought it time to intervene. 'And you've settled on Menu Two?' She had to double-check. Although even if Violette abruptly changed her mind Menu Two would still have to go ahead. 'All the food had been bought in.'

'Just let me check again,' Violette said, as though she suddenly saw Menu Two through different eyes.

Lilli rolled her blue orbs heavenwards. 'We've already settled on Menu Two, Vi. We can't mess Daniela around.'

'That's true.' Daniela smiled pleasantly. Why did Violette set out to be so odious? Lilli seemed to be coming around. There was hope for *her*. 'I think you've come up with the right choice,' she said, putting approval into her voice.

A chef's palate was his or her most crucial faculty. What separated a good cook from a chef was the understanding of food, the ability to bring together complex flavours and bring those flavours to a new dimension. An important part of her job was constantly tasting, refining, adjusting, innovating. It was this that years before had brought her to the attention of a famous French chef—that and her calm and careful temperament in a volatile environment. And it was the nod from that famous chef that had helped her jump a few rungs. Everything took time and concentration. She knew this menu worked. It might have been fun to try out some of the new 'molecular gastronomy', but the tried and true had its advantages—especially first-off.

'Menu Two' featured a tartare of ocean trout, served with fresh goat's cheese as an entrée; Sansho peppered chicken breasts with poached baby vegetables, shitake mushrooms and *foie gras velouté* as the main course, that was safe, followed by a fresh lime curd tart with a *crème fraîche* sorbet. She had even picked the wines to go with each course. The Denbys kept a fine cellar.

'Well…please don't do anything wrong, Daniela,' Violette warned as though terrible things might happen to her if she did. 'I'd be *most* unhappy if we had slip-ups.'

'Nothing at all will go wrong,' Daniela told her, with a confidence she didn't really feel. She couldn't rid herself of the idea that Violette had the whole thing rigged. But surely that was absurd?

'All the toffs have arrived,' Jules told them gleefully, as he swung back into the kitchen. He was relishing the occasion. 'Dressed to kill, the lot of 'em. Nothing like a party to make people shine. I've never worn a tux in my life. One guy out there looks exactly like James Bond—except our guy's got light eyes. Cat's eyes, I reckon. Hell, he looks good! The ladies think so, too.'

It wasn't difficult to guess who that was.

'Well, don't just stand there, boyo!' Gary broke in. 'It's all hands on deck.'

'Right you are, matey!' Jules, a handsome young man with thick flaxen hair gelled into the latest style and bright blue eyes, gave an impish grin.

Jules was to help Gary with the serving. Though young, Jules was a great mover, with nerves of steel and an enviable self-confidence. Daniela had refused Violette's request that she do the serving herself, saying that in all honesty her place was in the kitchen. No doubt Violette had had a little accident in mind, like landing a main dish in someone's lap. It was Daniela's practice, however, to make a brief appearance at the very end of the meal—minus her protective clothing—to ensure all had gone well.

Gary and Jules were dressed alike, in narrow black trousers and snowy white shirts, collarless and pintucked. They looked good. An A-grade student, Jules had disappointed his parents with his choice of a career. It had upset their plans.

They knew nothing about the food industry—and had wanted him to study law. Jules just wanted to become a cook.

Twenty minutes after it had been agreed that the guests would be seated at the dinner table, ready to be served the entrée, they were all still congregated in the drawing room, where they had been enjoying pre-dinner drinks. Daniela could feel herself getting upset. It wasn't easy to keep food at its peak. It needed to be served right on time.

'Are you sure everyone has arrived?' she double-checked with Gary. On rare occasions it happened that a guest was unavoidably late. Not everything went as planned.

'Did a head count,' Gary confirmed. 'All present and accounted for.'

'Have a quiet word in Violette's ear,' she told him, after another ten minutes had elapsed.

'She'd slap him if he got that close.' Jules gave another bad-boy grin.

'Do it all the same.'

To no avail. Instinctively Daniela *knew* Violette was counting on getting her out of the kitchen and into the drawing room, to do the reminding herself. Anything to cause a bit of embarrassment or, in Violette's view, bring her down a peg. Her most distinguished clients back in London, always the most considerate, would never have done this

to her. Their guests would have been gently shep-
herded into the dining room.

'Damn it!' Gary was getting angry now. 'I'm
starting to think this is deliberate. The woman
wants us to fall on our faces.'

'Try her one more time,' Daniela advised. 'Tell
her very quietly that if she and her guests don't go
to the table now, she might well be doing the
serving herself.'

'Good for you, Danni—call her bluff,' Jules
egged her on. 'Better yet, let *me* do it.'

Daniela waved that risky suggestion away,
shifting her attention to the food. She had made
the final touches to the entrée a good twenty
minutes before, but as it was a cold dish it could
stand for a while before it was ready to be eaten.
Even so the ocean trout mixture that had been
packed so gently within baking rings might lose
its precise shape.

The seasoned chicken breasts, sealed in a hot
frying pan, had been transferred to a pre-heated
oven. The poached baby vegetables could be kept
warm in the stock they were cooked in. She could
whiz the sauce a couple of times to keep it light
and frothy.

Violette heeded the warning, and they got
through the rest of the meal without incident.

Coffee and liqueurs had just been served, along

with some tiny dark chocolate confections Daniela had made especially, when Jules glided back into the kitchen, wearing an expression of concern. 'What's the matter with the flowers?' he asked.

Daniela stared at him. 'They're all right, aren't they?' What *could* go wrong with them?

'They've really wilted,' he said, drumming his fingers rather nervously on a benchtop. 'You didn't forget about the water?'

'Don't be stupid, Jules.' Gary reprimanded the boy without wanting to cause him too much discomfort. Jules had performed extremely well tonight, validating their confidence in him. He might easily have been in the business for years instead of six months.

Jules shook his trendily coiffed head. 'All I know is the ferns and the orchids in the swan have kind of keeled over through dinner. I'd say it won't be long before they're *dead*. One of the guests— the sweet little redhead, Zoe—' Jules's face momentarily lit '—was trying to fix them with her fingers. It was a sort of talking point. *Madam* looked very put out. Personally, I think Violette Denby looks wicked.'

Daniela felt herself go cold. 'The tiny orchids and the baby's breath around the candlesticks. Are they okay?'

'Spry as ever,' Jules nodded. 'And they don't

have *any* water. Anyone would think someone had poured some bleach into the swan.'

Gary glanced across at Daniela. 'Maybe *that's* her game?' he asked, his eyebrows coming together in anger and concern.

'Would *you* do such a thing at your own dinner party?' Daniela retorted.

Gary shrugged. 'Leave it to a jealous woman every time. She's giving that Mastermann guy the full treatment—matter of fact, all evening she's looked like she wanted to eat him, forget the menu. Or that's how I see it.'

Danielle barely heard. She was reflecting that she was the outsider here. Violette was on her home ground. She was a stunning-looking woman and she knew how to be charming when it suited her. The knowledge lay coiled like a snake in Daniela's chest.

Daniela made her brief appearance a short time later, in her little black dress. She wasn't sure what she'd expected, but the guests greeted her with much interest, enthusiasm, and lots of plaudits on the beautiful food and its presentation.

Carl, looking fantastically handsome in his evening clothes, came to her side, lowering his voice for her ears alone. 'Dinner was wonderful, Daniela,' he said warmly, looking smilingly into her eyes. 'Rest happy. As for the flowers in the swan…I'm not sure Violette hasn't been up to a few tricks.'

'It would certainly explain it,' Daniela murmured, immensely grateful he had made a point of coming to her.

'Such a pity about the orchids,' Zoe, the pretty redhead, came up to say. 'I expect the heat got to them.' Her voice conveyed nothing but sympathy and friendliness, no guile.

'I've never had such a thing happen before,' Daniela said regretfully, her eyes on the wilted arrangement, so cruelly robbed of its beauty. So much for any *heat*—a lovely breeze was coming in through the open French doors. The delicate white petals almost looked as if they'd been *burned*.

'Don't let it put you off,' Zoe whispered behind her hand. 'You won't be waiting long for the phone to ring. *Everyone* will want you. You're marvellous! Please don't go back to London early.'

Violette, her high-cheekboned face taut with anger, had no qualms at all about taking Daniela to task. The last of her guests had departed, and she clearly felt free to raise her voice.

Daniela felt a preparatory charge of adrenaline. This wasn't going to be pleasant.

'I hope you're not expecting the full amount of

your exorbitant fee?' was Violette's opening salvo. She seized hold of a piece of notepaper, shredding it violently as though it was the cheque Daniela was expecting.

Daniela gave her a very straight look, thinking how dumb she had been taking the job in the first place. 'I certainly am. My fee was agreed. All the guests I spoke to were perfectly happy with dinner.'

'Okay, so they were too kind to point out that the centrepiece was a disaster,' Violette said, her voice vindictive.

'And I can't quite fathom why. Perhaps it's time for you to tell me what *you* put in the water?' Why should she put up with this? Daniela thought. This strange young woman had gone out of her way to humiliate her.

For answer Violette flapped her hands wildly in the air, as though swatting a plague of flies. 'Are you mad?'

'Are *you*?' Daniela countered, thinking Violette might have brought herself to a new low. 'You were prepared to spoil your own dinner party to make *me* look bad. If that's not mad, please tell me what is?'

Violette's blue eyes flared with shock. She was about to reply, only there was a knock on the kitchen door.

Gary put his head around it. 'I'm off, Danni.

Everything okay?' His eyes went from the petite Daniela to the tall Violette, who for all her stunning good looks, seemed ready to kill.

'Fine.' Daniela gave him a reassuring smile. 'Ms Denby is just complimenting us on a splendid effort.'

Gary's round pleasant face looked highly dubious. 'Okay, then. I'll say goodnight.'

''Night, Gary.'

Violette shooed him off, her mood explosive.

'Actually, if you don't mind, I'll take a sample of the flower water and have it analysed,' Daniela said. 'I'm sure a chemist will do it for me.' It was an empty threat. She had no intention of doing any such thing, even if a chemist would oblige. But Violette must have believed her, because her haughty expression wavered.

'No, no—you'll do no such thing!' She placed her hands on her slim hips, standing tall. 'I'd like you out of here.'

Daniela gave a wry laugh, sitting down firmly on the nearest chair. 'Then we both want the same thing. But I'm not going anywhere without my cheque. Tell me, is there *sport* in doing what you do, Violette?' she asked, genuinely curious.

'I can't for the life of me think what you mean.' Violette's voice was so tight it had trouble making it out of her throat.

'Now who's kidding who? You were prepared to let the food go cold, and you sabotaged the arrangement—all as a way of embarrassing me. It didn't work. Though I hate to see those beautiful flowers deliberately ruined. Plus, they were very expensive.'

Violette didn't cave in. Not for a moment. 'Who would care?' she snapped, then swept out of the room, returning moments later, cheque in hand. 'You should be very grateful I'm giving you this,' she said, ice chunks for eyes.

'I'm not, particularly.' Daniela took the cheque, studying it as though it might be a dud. Violette couldn't be childish enough to stop payment, could she? 'I did my very best for you, Violette. Your guests went off happy. A few of them, however, might go home wondering what *really* happened to the orchids. What did you put in them, and when?'

Black storm clouds scudded across Violette's patrician face. 'I was as dismayed as everybody else. Certainly *Linc* thought you had slipped up somewhere. But I bet this isn't the first time you've messed up,' she said through clenched teeth.

Daniela nodded, refusing to believe Carl had thought—or said—any such thing. 'Sure, I've made mistakes. Who hasn't? But you're the one who had better pray no one finds out about your little trick. They might find it all too possible to believe.'

* * *

Linc sat in the darkness, in his parked car, sheltered by trees and blossoming shrubs. He was waiting for Daniela to appear. It seemed as if he had been waiting for her all his life. And now that she had come he would never let her go. Daniela Adami had become central to his plans. He not only desired her madly, he admired her immensely—not simply for her beauty and her intelligence, but for her driving force, her will to succeed. She had done so very, very well—for herself and for her family, who were rightfully proud of her. He was proud himself.

He had seen all the other guests leaving, followed some time later by the tall young fellow, Jules, who had served the truly memorable dinner like a pro, and then Gary. Just as he was wondering—and it had to be admitted worrying—what was taking Daniela so long, she came down the steps of the homestead, carrying a fairly large basket.

His heart flipped at the very sight of her. The familiar excitement gripped him. She could literally bring a man to his knees. She had made an appearance at the end of the evening in a little black dress, looking impeccable and, as far as he was concerned, putting every other woman in the shade. The more he thought about that business with the centerpiece, the clearer it became. The Denby sisters were escalating their campaign.

Violette had only hired Daniela to find some way to embarrass her. He had the dismal feeling *he* was at the bottom of things, as the latest eligible male in the valley. There were a lot more unstable people around than one would think. Violette could well turn out to be one of them…

He hopped out of his car, lengthening his stride to get to Daniela. 'Here—let me take that.' He reached for the white basket filled with various items she had needed for the night. The weight meant nothing to him, but it was probably heavy for her. 'I was getting worried.' He glanced down on her. Even at night the bell of her hair shone.

'I didn't think you would stay,' she said, enormously gratified he had.

'What, and not follow you safely home? Something's the matter, isn't it?' His eyes never left her. He was so attuned to her he could read her body language even in the dark.

'No, everything's okay.' They had reached her small car now, and Daniela was trying to organise her chaotic thoughts. She opened the boot and Linc swung the basket in.

'It's no use telling me that, Daniela.' His voice was openly sceptical.

'You can read me like a book?' She looked up at him. He had taken off his dinner jacket and his white shirt gleamed in the indigo darkness.

Superbly tall and lean, he was, to her, the epitome of male power and grace.

But he laughed harshly. 'Not entirely. I do have an idea you and Violette might have had words. I mean, she deliberately held up dinner. I wasn't the only one to notice. That Zoe is a sharp little thing, and a few of the others. Then there was the business with the flowers. God knows when she picked her moment.'

'All in a day's work,' she said calmly, but in the next instant her temper spurted. 'I was a plain fool accepting the job. At least I know she'll never call on me again.'

'I'm pretty sure none of her friends will join her,' he said dryly. 'Everyone enjoyed dinner immensely. Let's get out of here,' he said. 'Someone is looking through the curtain. I think it's Lilli. I saw her give her sister a few hard looks. There are a lot of similarities, but Lilli has the potential to be a whole lot nicer free of her sister's influence.'

It was Daniela's opinion as well. 'Nevertheless, she's keeping an eye on you now, with a view to reporting back to Violette. *You'd better get over here. She's talking to Linc.*'

'Mightn't that work for us?' he asked swiftly. 'Their seeing us together? Neither of them mean anything to me, Daniela.'

'That's sad when they both want you.'

He could hardly deny it. Linc drew in a deep slow breath. 'I'm sure I haven't given either of them the slightest encouragement, beyond a bit of tomfoolery at Guy's wedding. Certainly no serious business. A lot of women hanker after what they can't get.'

She responded sharply to the note in his voice. 'You're speaking from experience?'

'I'm just laying it on the line,' he answered, his voice terse.

She moved to the front of her car, ready to unlock the door on the driver's side. 'It would hardly surprise me to hear a lot of women have hankered after you.'

He gave a laugh, a sardonic glint in his eyes. 'What does a man do to avoid them?'

That gave her pause. Hadn't she done everything in her power to avoid Gerald Templeton, without success? 'Look, it's one o'clock in the morning,' she said, determined not to be the kind of woman ripe for the plucking. 'You don't have to follow me, Carl. Fly away home. I'm fine.'

He rested his hand over hers, tightening it slightly, stirring up all her senses to something like anguish. 'You're really not. Come back with me. Please.'

She could feel herself starting to tremble. In all other things she could keep her emotions under restraint. With him she was demonstratively passionate. He was the one who had unlocked her sensuality. 'I don't want to do that,' she said, knowing how half-hearted it sounded.

'It's odd, but I don't believe you. That's *exactly* what you want to do.'

She rounded on him with unconscious seductiveness. 'You're so sure of yourself, aren't you?'

'You'll have to do better than that, Daniela.' He rested his hands on her delicate shoulders. Every part of her body was lovely—her hands and her feet. He wondered for the very first time what a child of theirs would look like. A little girl, with her mother's wondrous beauty and spirit. 'If you're upset—and you are—I really want to hear about it. And afterwards I want to make it up to you.'

'In bed?' Her honeyed voice bit, though her yearning was sharp.

'Can you think of a better way?' he retorted, wanting to pull her into his arms, but aware that Lilli was probably still watching from upstairs, believing herself unobserved. 'Don't let's argue,' he said, looking down at her intently. 'Come back with me—if only for a little while.' Very gently he touched her cheek, letting his finger trail down to her swanlike neck.

Their eyes met. He lowered his dark head, nuzzling the side of that neck softly. She tilted her head so as to better accept his caressing mouth. It was impossible not to surrender to the spell.

Believing herself screened by the curtain, Lilli continued to look down into the drive, her stomach tied in knots. The exterior lights were still on, so she could see their dusky silhouettes. She couldn't have moved even if she had wanted to. She was caught up in what was happening down there.

The death of her dreams, she thought dramatically, though in her heart of hearts she had known she had no chance.

The exterior lights hit their figures obliquely. He was facing the house, towering over the petite Daniela, his white shirt gleaming. She saw him take Daniela's shoulders. She saw the way he lowered his head to kiss her cheek, or her throat— she couldn't quite make out which, but she wished to God it was happening to *her*. Linc Mastermann was the kind of guy to drive a girl wild.

Moments later both of them got into their cars, Daniela leaving first. Lilli slowly dropped her hand from the curtain. She had a vivid image of them together. *Naked*. In bed. She knew the way he would make love would be unforgettable.

'What the devil are you doing?'

Violette's loud voice startled her so much she jumped.

'For crying out loud, what are you trying to do? Shatter glass? What does it look like?' Lilli croaked, made to feel like a sneak by someone who had made sneakiness an art form. '*He* waited for her.'

Violette's rage overflowed. 'He *wh-a-t*?' She broke off, speechless, stalking to the window. 'There's no one there.' She turned on Lilli, as though Lilli were delusional.

'They've gone.' Lilli stood a distance away, a beautiful, sadly disappointed young woman in her lovely lilac satin dress. 'You've yet to learn how to play it smart, Vi,' she said with regret in her voice. 'That bit with the flowers was just plain dumb. What did you spray them with? I can just see you ransacking the kitchen cupboard.'

'Don't be so ridiculous,' Violette shot back savagely. It was Violette's way to deny everything she didn't want to face.

Despite her wretched disappointment Lilli laughed. 'Hey, it's *me*, remember? Your sister. The last person in the world to trust you. Hell, I remember the tricks you used to play on Alana. That didn't stop her from landing Guy. Now you want to play your little tricks on Daniela.'

'And what evidence do you have to support

this?' Violette demanded in her most crushing Big-Sister voice.

'The evidence of our whole lives flashing before our eyes,' Lilli answered quietly. 'Remember that girl—the scholarship girl—Fiona Scott at school? Poor old Fiona! Didn't you cause *her* some grief! You've been a bad influence on me, Vi. You've made me do a whole lot of things I didn't want to do. I've been gutless. Too easily led. Okay, I took a real shine to Linc. What girl wouldn't? He's gorgeous. You felt the same. Only *one* problem—and it's huge. Daniela is the one he's interested in.'

'Daniela who's going back to London, or have you forgotten?' Violette retorted, absolutely seething at her sister's disloyalty.

'I'll believe that when it happens,' Lilli replied. 'My advice is save yourself for another guy. There must be someone out there who doesn't know or hasn't heard you're so horrid. I'm going back to Sydney tomorrow.'

'Good!' Violette responded hotly. 'Then we might be able to get a bit of peace around here.'

CHAPTER EIGHT

A COUPLE of weeks later Daniela took a call from Florence, the birthplace of the Renaissance. It was Alana, sounding absolutely on top of the world, her voice as clear as if she was ringing from Sydney. Daniela had received two postcards from the honeymooners, one from Paris, another from Rome, and now she was delighted to take the call.

The two young women chatted for a few minutes, with Alana filling her in on all the wonderful sights she had seen. She raved about the Uffizi, one of the world's most splendid art galleries, and said the food was to die for. Their honeymoon was the experience of a lifetime. But Guy wanted to talk to Daniela. Alana handed over the phone.

Guy's smooth cultured voice came on the line. They talked for a little while, and then Guy sprang his big surprise. His chef, Lee, at the Winery Restaurant, needed to return home to Hong Kong as soon as possible. His father, who had been in poor health for some time, was declining and his ageing mother needed him to be on hand. He estimated he would need to be away a month, maybe a little longer. Would Daniela be interested in taking over the position of Executive Chef in his absence? There were two chefs under Lee, and they would be remaining in place. They could handle most weekdays. It was the Friday and Saturday nights Guy was most concerned with. He named a figure no chef would turn down, but didn't expect Daniela to consent on the spot. He would give her another day to decide.

The offer was very tempting. At the Winery Restaurant she could go beyond the norm, which was to say the menus could be far more creative than what she was currently planning at the family bistro. She immediately thought of French-Japanese combinations, or her own interpretation of Japanese food. Her style was drawn from French origins—after all, she had received her training in Paris—and she understood the French kitchen. Although even Japanese chefs described themselves as French chefs.

The Winery had a full client list. If one wanted a table a reservation had to be made well in advance. It would be a challenge, but first she would have to speak to her parents, who were pretty much relying on her to come up with the kind of dishes that kept customers flowing into the bistro. Then again, she could overcome that problem by formulating written menus and instructions without actually doing the cooking herself. Her parents had been amazingly quick to pick up on her techniques. Whatever she had asked, they had done very well—if not the first time, then certainly the second. The *sous chefs* at the Winery had to be first class, with a high level of technique, and the chances that she could do a lot of directing those without actually having to demonstrate were excellent.

It wasn't her habit to write things down, but she could easily make a start. When Guy rang late the following afternoon she said what he was hoping to hear—yes.

Gerald had hired a car in Sydney, then followed the route to the Hunter Valley—which he had to admit was beautiful. So much so, he made a stop overnight to sample the best of the food and the wine. Surprisingly good. This was his first trip to Australia—the far end of the world. They had the climate and Sydney Harbour, but he had not been prepared for just how much more Australia offered. Sydney was a flourishing metropolis, a world-class city, blessed with the magnificent harbour and glorious beaches within easy reach.

He had even been impressed by the massive Sydney Harbour Bridge and the Opera House that occupied a prominent harbourside position. He'd had an excellent view from his luxury hotel.

Nevertheless it was beyond bizarre that his Daniela would want to bury herself not in the metropolis, but in the sticks. This Wangaree Valley, his destination, was still farther on from the Hunter. Who in their right mind would leave London and all it had to offer for a rural valley on the other side of the world, no matter how beautiful and prosperous? There was no logic to it. Rome he might have believed. Not some place called Wangaree Valley, which he had been told was something of a stronghold for the descendants of Australia's sheep barons.

He had led this conversation at Reception, and the very attractive brunette behind the desk had been most forthcoming with information. He had always had a way with women. She had even named a prominent family in the area, the Radcliffes. For a sickening moment his mind had jumped to a connection between Daniela and a Radcliffe, only in the next breath the brunette had told him Guy Radcliffe, the current owner of Wangaree Station, had recently married a girl called Alana Caulfield…Calloway—something like that.

It should be very easy to find her. For the past

couple of months he had been unable to think of anything but finding Daniela. One couldn't lose a woman like that without feeling a tremendous jolt. In his thirty-two years of life he had never experienced anything like what he felt for Daniela. He had even come around to the idea of marrying her, if that was what she wanted. His frame of mind hadn't lent itself to his work. He wasn't raking in the usual commissions. Finally the head of the firm, who just happened to be his uncle Philip, had told him to take a break.

'I can't let you handle anything of significance, Gerald. There's something on your mind. Go ahead and sort yourself out.'

Some part of him registered he had treated Daniela badly. Obviously she had become deeply disturbed by his habit of turning up wherever she was, and by the silent phone calls. There was nothing he could do about all that. It had happened. What he had to do now was convince her he had changed. That she had the chance of a wonderful life with him on a grander scale than anything she could possibly aspire to. Offer marriage. Even his difficult to impress mother had commented on how truly beautiful Daniela was. *And such an air!* Daniela should ask herself this question: where would she find better?

* * *

After his mother had died so tragically young, Linc had doubted he would ever find true happiness again, find that wonderful contentment he had felt as a boy when he was with his mother. She had been so lovely, so sunny-natured, so full of fun and understanding. Such women were unforgettable. His mother had been taken from him and Chuck, and after her death their father had rarely spoken her name. His dad was one of those men who had to do the macho thing and have little flutters on the side, but he had genuinely loved his wife. That was until her illness had robbed her of her health and her beauty.

Linc was sure his dad didn't love Cheryl. What he felt for Cheryl was lust, pure and simple—plus there was the bonus of having a glamorous young wife on his arm. That meant something to his dad and men like him. Maybe they felt driven to prove something? Either way, he didn't admire his dad. He wished he did, but he didn't. End of story.

His own relationship with Daniela had changed everything. Suddenly he was feeling on top of the world. Full of zest, full of plans. Both of them were working extremely hard—he at Briar's Ridge, where he slogged until his body ached. He had taken on a middling enterprise. He intended to make it big. And Daniela had taken on the job of Executive Chef at Guy's Winery Restaurant.

She was pulling in even bigger crowds, some coming from as far away as Sydney. She had spoken to him about it before giving Guy her answer. Her family hadn't wanted to spoil her chances. Neither did he. The only problem was they had less and less time together, so what they did have was doubly precious.

Tonight he was driving into town to her apartment. A quiet dinner; just the two of them. *Perfect.* His heart literally danced in his chest, pulses thrumming like guitars in his ears. They would talk about all that had been happening to them— both of them took a great interest in what the other was doing—and afterwards they would make love. He had never thought of sex as being as addictive as a powerful drug but he was sure what he and Daniela shared together must be on that level. The natural progression from that, in his view, was marriage. He didn't just want to share a table and a bed with her. He wanted to share his entire life. He wanted her to be the mother of his children. Their children would be a mix of them. They would love them to bits and bring them up right.

He knew in his heart his mother would approve his choice. But neither he nor Daniela had discussed the future, so he decided it was high time to prepare the way. He wasn't going to rush her. There were still some of his questions she wouldn't answer, but he truly believed there was a future for them. How could he let go of this miracle in his life?

He had his own key to her apartment. Even if there were times she was late arriving home, he could always let himself in.

Carl usually arrived right on time. Tonight he was a good twenty minutes early. She didn't mind in the least. She couldn't wait to see him. There were so many things she wanted to tell him. Get everything out in the open. No secrets between them. Instinct told her there was something in his relationship with his stepmother she needed reassuring about. She knew how certain people could scar you. Maybe, like herself, Carl had put himself out of reach of a person who could hurt him.

Swiftly she removed the apron that protected her pretty dress and hurried out into the small foyer, responding to his knock. Clearly he was having trouble finding his keys. She threw open the door, a lovely welcoming smile on her face.

Instantly she lost it. The past had reached out and caught up with her.

Gerald Templeton stood outside her door—handsome, debonair, immaculately dressed, dark wavy hair barbered to perfection, an answering smile on his face. He was carrying a sheaf of long-stemmed red roses which he tried to urge into her nerveless arms.

'Gerald, go away!' she cried in a low throbbing tone. 'I don't want this. I have absolutely nothing to say to you.' Hadn't she left London feeling emotionally stripped?

His chiselled face and the soft upper-class voice were full of pleading. 'Daniela, listen—*please*!'

'No way.' After the way he had persecuted her? She went to shut the door, but he forcibly held it open.

'I know this is a tremendous surprise,' he said quickly, a lot of emotions struggling in his good-looking face. 'Please don't send me away. I should have let you know I was coming. I'm in Australia on business and I thought it might be better this way—face to face. How are you? You look more beautiful than ever. Please let me in for a moment. Is that so much to ask? Please, Daniela, *please*. Can't we talk?'

Life returned to her limbs. 'I don't know how you found me, Gerald,' she responded tautly, 'but it should have become obvious, even to you, that I didn't want to be found. I'll ask you again to go away.'

He tried a smile, as though this might calm her down. 'Good lord, you wouldn't want to get rid of me so easily, would you? I've come all this way—mostly to apologise for what an insensitive brute I was. I have no excuse except to say I was temporarily off my head. I couldn't bear for our relationship to end, especially the way it did. All I'm asking is a few minutes of your time. I think you'll find it worth your while.'

Now the familiar arrogance was back in play. 'Believe that and you'll believe anything, Gerald,' she said. 'I accept your apology. Your behaviour *was* both appalling and threatening. Now I'd like you to go. I have a guest who will be arriving at any minute.'

'You're cooking dinner?' Despite himself, he couldn't keep the lash of jealousy out of his voice. He could smell the delicious aromas, but that gave him no pleasure. Of course she was cooking dinner. For a *man*. There would always be a man.

She turned her head briefly over her shoulder. 'Yes. So—'

She got no further.

He pushed his way in, casting the beautiful, fragrant roses aside and grasping her arm, compelling her into the living room.

'Get away from me!' Daniela cried, breaking free, horrified by his actions.

'Daniela, calm down—please calm down,' he begged, his expression imploring. 'The last thing in the world I would do is hurt you. How could you think that? I'm here to ask you to marry me.'

'Oh, my God!'

His dark eyes lit. He stared back at her, waiting. Even to his own ears the offer was mind-blowing. She was probably swept off her feet. 'You know you're very fond of me. What we had was good. Given a little time, I know I can make you love me.'

She knew she was under threat. Gerald might look as respectable as they came, but he was unstable. 'You must be insane,' she said. 'You can't *make* me do anything. What about your fiancée? Lady Laurella? Or have you lost her as well?'

Gerald studied her, told her to sit down. Daniela remained on her feet. 'Laurella had my parents' backing,' he said. 'I thought I needed her, but I find I don't. I was trying to please the parents. I've thought this through and through, Daniela. I'm here to beg you to forgive me. I want you to come back with me. We're meant to be together.'

He reached for her, but Daniela's temper, that she had spent her lifetime keeping under control, flared out of bounds. She wasn't frightened any more. Carl would come. Carl would take care of Gerald Templeton. Everything would be all right.

Linc left in plenty of time to make the drive into town. He was halfway there when he came on an accident. A small car had run off the road and hit a tree. A 4WD was parked on the opposite side of the road. The occupants, he guessed, were the middle-aged couple several feet from the crashed car. He picked up the scene in his headlights. There was no way he could glide past.

He stopped on the steep verge and applied the handbrake. 'Has an ambulance been called?' He moved swiftly to look inside the car. He checked the ignition was off. A young fellow was slumped against the wheel, mercifully alive, but moaning in pain. There was blood on his face, his head, and down the front of his shirt. He didn't respond when Linc spoke to him, asking how badly he thought he was hurt. To make matters worse Linc had no difficulty picking up the reek of alcohol.

The woman came up to Linc, a sensible-looking countrywoman. 'We rang the ambulance right away. He's hardly more than a child. Been drinking, it seems. He must have been speeding and lost control of the wheel. You're the new owner of Briar's Ridge, aren't you?'

'That's right, ma'am. Linc Mastermann.'

'Marjorie Beecham.' She introduced her husband, Alan, who had joined them. The husband, much older, looked very shaken. 'We were just on our way back home,' he said. 'We saw it happen.'

'I don't think we should move him,' Linc said, thinking there could be internal injuries, at least a broken rib.

'That's what we thought,' Mrs Beecham replied. 'Might do more harm than good.'

As they were speaking the ambulance arrived, making a U-turn and then parking in front of Linc's car. A weight of anxiety was taken off their minds. They stayed until the young man had been checked over, then put into the ambulance. The ambulance driver sketched a salute, hopped in the vehicle, then moved off.

The upshot was that Linc was late arriving at Daniela's apartment. He locked his car, then took a step back, glancing up at her floor. The balcony lights were on, flooding over an array of plants and a prolifically flowering white bougainvillaea in a glossy ceramic pot. He would let himself in.

Impetuously he bounded in and out of the empty lift, filled with a wonderful sense of well-being. He moved fast down the corridor, his body language expressing a real sense of purpose and his urgency to see her. He wanted to hold her face in his hands. He wanted to kiss her until she was swooning in his arms.

He tapped on the door first to alert her of his arrival, then unlocked it, calling, 'It's me.' Almost at once he knew something was wrong. 'Daniela?'

She usually hurried out to greet him. His eyes fell on a sheaf of red roses that looked as if they had been tossed on the floor. The head of a rose had broken off, to roll a short distance away. Now, that was distinctly odd.

'Daniela?' At once he was as tense as a jungle cat, his muscles coiled to spring.

'It's all right, Carl.'

Sudden relief swept through him. Her voice had come from the bedroom.

'You scared me,' he called, walking down the passageway. 'You shouldn't do that.' Even as he moved, he tried to think it through. Her voice had sounded different…strained? Then there were the roses. One would hardly leave roses lying on the floor. That bothered him.

The bedroom door was half shut. He pushed it open, at the same time keeping well back against the wall. Two people were in the room. Daniela was standing at the far side of the room, arms wrapped protectively around herself; a tall, suavely handsome guy stood immobilised opposite her. The bed was fully made up with a gold silk brocade quilt and an array of silk cushions. It was the only barrier between them.

'What the hell?' Linc asked discordantly. He felt stupefied for a moment, none too certain what was going on.

Daniela moved very quickly around the bed, rushing to his side. She was very pale, her dark eyes huge in her face. 'I knew you'd come.'

He seized her with one arm around her waist, holding her to him. He could feel the trembling that ran right through her body. All the while he kept staring at the other man. 'So who are *you*?' He addressed himself directly to Daniela's visitor, a guy who looked absolutely trustworthy, though it was abundantly clear Daniela didn't trust him at all.

The man cleared his throat. 'Gerald Templeton.' He identified himself as though his name must be distinguished enough to allay anyone's fears. He glanced down at his watch. 'I expect I should be on my way. I had an appointment fifteen minutes ago.'

Daniela drew even closer to Linc.

'What's he doing here, Daniela?' Linc asked tightly, deliberately blocking Templeton's exit. He needed to find out what this was all about. Templeton looked fit, around six feet, a few years older than him by the look of it, but Linc knew he was strong enough to defend himself if necessary.

'Easily explained,' Templeton broke in, aware the other man, impressively tall and in wonderful shape, was on trigger alert. 'I'm in Sydney on business. I thought as I was so close I'd call on Daniela. We saw quite a bit of each other in London.'

Realisation slotted in. 'So you're the guy who

was harassing her?' Linc asked, silver-green eyes narrowing with menace.

Templeton responded to the implied threat. His head fell, not in contrition, more as an indication of deep betrayal. 'Is that what she's been telling you?'

'Come on.' Linc threw him a disgusted, challenging look. 'You were giving her a lot of trouble.'

Templeton looked up, his mouth twisting in a grimace. 'Sorry—it was the other way around. Look, I don't want to say any more. It will only make matters worse. I just came here to ask Daniela to marry me.'

'And you were going to make yourself comfortable in the bedroom while you were doing the asking?' Linc's eyes fairly blazed in his face. He was trying his best to understand, but he was having more trouble than he thought. Clearly this guy was genuinely in love with Daniela.

Templeton appeared to be bracing himself against all insult. 'When Daniela left London she knew things weren't over between us.'

'And you were giving her a little breathing space? Is that it?' Linc was still searching the other man's face in an effort to divine what was really going on.

Daniela shook her head frantically. 'Carl—please.'

Both men ignored her.

'The answer is yes!' Templeton's voice rang with sincerity. 'I love her and she loves me.'

'If she only knew it.' Linc's laugh was harsh, his fists clenching of their own volition. The anger and confusion that was in him was cresting. Daniela had never fully explained her relationship with this man who had so inopportunely turned up. He looked civilised enough, only Daniela's reactions were telling him something was very wrong.

Now Templeton appealed to Daniela—full of passion and turmoil. 'Aren't you going to say something, darling?' he begged. 'Tell your... friend here, every word I've spoken is the truth. I *did* come here to ask you to marry me?'

'Why don't you just go, Gerald?' Daniela said, her voice dropping to a whisper as she was overcome by a spasm of weakness. Carl had arrived not a moment too soon.

Incredibly, there were tears in Templeton's dark eyes. 'You won't come back with me? You're upset now. I can come again tomorrow.'

'Don't even think about it,' Linc warned, gripping Daniela tighter. 'There have been some big changes around here, Gerald.' He glanced down at Daniela, oddly silent within the curve of his arm. 'I take it you haven't told him?'

'Told me what?' Templeton's eyes riveted themselves to Daniela's face.

'Think, man,' Linc said crisply. 'How can Daniela accept your proposal when she's already accepted mine?'

There was a stunned silence, then Templeton burst out in rage. 'How could you do this to me?' he cried. 'Leading me a fine dance.' He was boiling with fury. 'Coming to Australia was just a stunt to get me to follow you, wasn't it? You wanted to bring me to heel.' His eyes shot to Linc. 'This is one sick girl,' he said, his voice packed with warning and the bitterest disappointment. 'She keeps it hidden, but you'll find out soon enough.'

Linc's face showed no emotion whatsoever, so tight was his self-control. 'How did you get here, Templeton?' he asked.

'I drove—what else?' Templeton thrust a hand violently through his thick dark hair.

'So your car's in the street?'

Templeton nodded, looking like a man who had been dealt a mortal blow. 'Even after everything you've done to me I can't hate you,' he said, his eyes settling once more on Daniela's beautiful face as though mesmerised.

'Why don't I see you to your car?' Linc suggested in a voice that brooked no refusal. 'I have a few questions.'

'And I'll answer them, so help me God!' Templeton let out a strangled breath. 'My beau-

tiful Daniela! I would have given you the world!'
He made a visible attempt to pull himself
together. 'At least I might be able to stop
someone else from putting himself through the
same hell I went through.'

'That's not the way it was, Gerald,' Daniela
said, raising her head.

'I loved you with my whole heart and soul.'
Templeton took several steps towards her, the set
of his handsome features ennobled in grief.

'Done. You're done now.' Linc stopped him in
his tracks by putting out an arm and steering him
backwards. 'I've heard more than enough. You
have to leave. *Now*.' He extended an imperative
arm to shepherd the other man from the room.

As far as Linc was concerned the evening
seemed to have shape-shifted itself into a disaster.
What had they been doing talking in the bedroom
anyway? Why not the living room? What would
it have taken for Templeton to get her into bed?
Okay, that made no sense at all. Daniela had
known he would be arriving. What she hadn't
known was that Templeton was going to ask her
to marry him. He'd seen the guy—the smooth,
handsome image—heard his voice. English upper
class. Social background meant a lot to them. Was
it possible Daniela had been hanging out for
marriage, as Templeton had claimed? Was

Daniela a witch who lived to put men under her spell? He couldn't sustain a thought like that. It was so disloyal.

Sunk in despair, her nerves jangling, Daniela began to put food back in the refrigerator. She covered the salad and mustard seed dressing. The escalopes of tuna to be served with mushrooms and witlof had only to be put under the grill. And Carl loved lime tart, so she had used a classic recipe. But who could eat in this state? She could just imagine what Gerald would be telling Carl. How would he know what were lies and what was real? Gerald was very convincing…

It was to have been a wonderful night. She had realised finally she had to tell Carl the truth about what had happened to drive her to find sanctuary back home. Gerald Templeton had been her worst nightmare. His handsome façade had hidden deep character flaws she had come to find repellent. Until Carl had arrived tonight she had been truly frightened. When Gerald had forced her to go with him to the bedroom her very scalp had crawled. What had he intended to do? She had repeated vehemently that she had a guest arriving. Yes, a *man*, she'd confirmed. A superbly fit young man, who would never permit her to be harmed. It was *he* who should be worried. Yet Gerald hadn't appeared fully capable of taking that in. Or had he thought he could deal with any male guest simply by opening the door and telling him to go away? Gerald's arrogance was unbelievable. She couldn't shake the sense he had intended to use force if need be to get her to agree to what he wanted. What he wanted was *her*.

She gulped down the rest of the glass of Riesling she had been sipping while preparing the meal. It had gone off the chill. She knew Gerald would spread his lies, doing everything in his power to convince Carl she had worked her way into his life, seduced him into falling in love with her and then, when he didn't immediately offer marriage, she had thrown down an ultimatum by fleeing to Australia. Gerald was clever, highly plausible. A by-product of his privileged life was the belief that he could have anything he wanted.

When Carl returned her heart flipped a double beat. 'He's gone?'

Carl, looking grim, threw himself onto a sofa, his expression dark. 'God!' he said soberly. 'How long did you know this guy?'

'A few months.'

'Please…don't hold back.' His extraordinary eyes were aglitter.

She slid down into an armchair, thinking her

legs were about to give way on her. 'I'm guessing he said longer?'

'He said you were together a year.'

'He was *lying*!' The words burst from her. She might feel like it, but she wasn't about to dissolve in tears. 'We were *never* together in the way he wanted. And I didn't sleep with him, if that's what you want to know?'

'*Were* you waiting for him to propose marriage?' Was that possible? Linc stared across at her. She was wearing a dress new to him, in a shade of red that was perfect with her golden complexion. He didn't think any man could want a woman more. 'It's a ploy that's worked since Anne Boleyn,' he suggested, with a sardonic shrug.

She shook her head sadly. 'I thought you knew me better than that. There's a devil in Gerald. I missed it completely when we first met. He was— well, you saw him. Gerald looks the quintessential English gentleman. We had dinner a number of times. We went to concerts, the theatre, art galleries. He took me down to his parents' country home, a very impressive place.'

'Sounds like he wanted you to meet them.' Linc watched the play of emotions on her beautiful face. Her stress was palpable. And because of the strength of his feeling for her his sexual jealousy had been unleashed.

'Not at all. A party was going on, and I was aware Gerald's parents had a suitable bride lined for him—a Lady Laurella Marks, one of his own circle. What Gerald had in mind for me was the role of mistress. Let's see—mistresses were invented long before Anne Boleyn, weren't they?' Now her soft honeyed voice held a trace of bitterness.

'He said you were lovers.' Not long after that he had hit Templeton's sneering, abruptly coarse mouth.

'Don't you think I would have told you if we were?' Her dark eyes were brilliant with unshed tears.

'Daniela, you haven't told me much at all.' He sighed. 'How does a man get to be obsessed with a woman when he hasn't even made love to her?'

Colour flamed in her cheeks. 'I didn't say he hadn't made love to me. It stopped short of sex.'

'Were you teasing him? Goading him?' There were so many images in his mind.

That hurt like an open wound. 'No. I was becoming increasingly uneasy about him. It got to the point he was ringing me—checking up on me—sometimes twelve times a day. He once accused me of starting an affair with a friend of his. He couldn't have been more wrong. It didn't seem to mean anything to him that his friend was married—happily married, I might add. To Gerald there was a certain cachet in having a loving wife and an exhilarating mistress. Why are you so angry anyway? You appear to have fallen for his lies.'

His eyes glinted. 'Not at all, but I'm feeling a little lost, and I have to admit jealous. Anyway it's becoming plain he was trying to poison *our* relationship.'

'Which is?' she asked quietly.

'Well, we *are* sleeping together.' He found himself responding to the turbulence in the air.

That hurt, too. 'Tell me about your step-mother?' she retaliated. *He* was the one who had opened the envelope. See how *he* reacted. 'Or are you afraid to?'

Linc thumped a hand on the arm of the sofa. 'Don't be ridiculous.' A muscle twitched along his taut jawline.

'You're not fond of her? *Too* fond of her?' *I mustn't do this. It's crazy!*

'I loathe her,' Linc muttered between his fine white teeth.

'But she doesn't loathe you?' Jealousy appeared to be driving them both.

That upset Linc. He had done everything in his power to give Cheryl a wide berth. 'Why talk about Cheryl? She isn't a part of this. Perhaps I ought to go?' He stood up, knowing the evening had been ruined but somehow unable to save it.

Templeton had said things that had really got under his skin. No wonder his temper had got the better of him.

'Please yourself.' Daniela rose as well, her surface antagonism hiding a wealth of hurt feelings. Gerald had afflicted them both with his venom. 'But go and you don't come back,' she said, in the full bloom of upset.

For a moment he didn't answer, and then he came slowly towards her. 'You know, I think you're really, *really* clever.'

She threw up her chin, her dark eyes brilliant with anger. 'What do you mean?'

'These ultimatums,' he said.

'You don't trust me?'

Why the hell didn't he confirm his trust in her? Jealousy was such a dangerous thing. It made a man say things he shouldn't. 'You're *my* witch,' he said. 'Why not Templeton's? Besides, you obviously don't trust *me.*'

'Then mightn't it be a good time to call it a day?' Sadness suddenly enveloped her like a cloud. Men stuck together. Woman was the temptress of choice.

She stared away and Linc took her by the shoulders, overwhelmed by her closeness and hating what was happening. 'Is that what you want? Talk to me, Daniela,' he pleaded. 'I'm crazy about you. You know that. But you confuse me.'

She threw up her head, tears in her eyes.

'Why do you cry? *Why?*' The hunger in him surged out of bounds. He could feel it all through his body, his heart, his lungs and his chest.

'I'm *not* crying,' she said, setting her delicate jaw. 'How can you possibly care about me and yet be ready to believe an unstable man like Gerald Templeton?' she accused him. 'I fled a great job, friends, to come home and escape him. He made my life a nightmare. He rang my phone endlessly and never spoke. He was somewhere there, wherever I was. Across the street, in the same building, in shops, parked in the street where I lived. You can't know what it was like!' She drew a long shuddering breath as disturbing memories hit her afresh.

A vertical line split Linc's black brows. 'You could have got a restraining order,' he said reasonably.

'You think that would have kept him away? His name carries weight in the City. Who was *I*? Besides, unstable people follow rules of their own. Do you know how many wives, girlfriends have taken out restraining orders only to be beaten up or killed? Some men are brutes. Don't for a minute think the upper classes are excluded. Gerald was brought up to believe he could have anything he liked. Certainly any woman. He wasn't a womaniser, but he wanted *me*. I desperately wanted to be left alone. That's why I had to move away. He could come back, for all I know.'

A truly daunting expression crossed Linc's face. 'He *won't* be coming back.' He spoke emphatically. 'Men like Templeton see women as helpless victims, easy marks. Essentially they're bullies on some sort of power kick. Templeton won't want to stick around here while I'm on the scene. You can be sure of that.'

'You told him you'd proposed to me.' She didn't look at him as she said it. She didn't know where they were any more.

'I did.' Linc nodded briskly. 'And I told him it really wouldn't be worth his while if he ever came near you again. I honestly think he paid attention.'

She had to force herself to move away. 'I feel sick, Linc. I think you should go.'

He grieved for the friction between them. He certainly wasn't about to leave her. 'Sorry. I'm staying here,' he said quietly. 'I won't bother you in any way. I can sleep on the couch. I just want you to know I'm here with you.' He was silent for a moment, then he burst out, 'Hell, I'm hungry. Let me put something together for you. It might make you feel better. I was so looking forward to tonight.'

'So was I.' Her gaze went to the roses that Gerald had pitched to the floor. 'Now it's destroyed.'

'I won't let you say that!' Linc's voice was full of intensity. 'Men like Templeton set out to be destroyers. They can't achieve their aims if you don't let them. Let's settle down, Daniela. *Please*. I could do with a drink. Let me get you one, too.'

Linc took a long time going to sleep. It wasn't just that his tall frame was way too long for the sofa—it sure was. It was more that he was wound up so tight it was damned near impossible to unwind. How could he when he was desperately trying to subdue what Daniela might see as the brute or the beast in him? No getting away from it—some of the male of the species had a brutal streak.

He could have kissed her, to the point where her own sexual needs were too driving to be refused. He knew he could have done that. On the other hand he knew he wouldn't. That would make him no better than Templeton, with his sick fantasies. The sooner it was morning the better. Maybe both of them needed to take a step away. Or maybe—he groaned—they needed to get closer. He only had to walk down the corridor, but he loved her too much.

Loved her?

Isn't that it, Mastermann? You love her. Nothing can change that.

* * *

He awoke with a start, his body tensed up.
'Daniela!' He wrenched himself halfway up, abs
and chest tight. 'Are you okay?'

She was bending over him, her hand on his
shoulder. 'I couldn't sleep,' she said, in her soft,
mellifluous voice.

God, the *sweetness* of her! She had come to
him. Felt the need. That thrilled him to the core.

She started to crawl over him, her hands
seeking his face, the ridges of his cheekbones, the
line of his jaw, then slipping down to his chest,
clawing on a whorl of hair. Her touch was electric.
Impulses were shooting all over his body. He
could no longer hold off. He hauled her onto his
lap, tilting her head back over his arm and burying
his face against her throat. The flavour of her skin
was exquisite. She was wearing a nightgown, a
mist of a thing, and his seeking hands, desperate
to touch her all over, told him she wore nothing
beneath it.

'I w-want you so much,' he stammered, his
strong hands trembling with emotion. 'I'm sorry
about earlier. I overreacted. I—'

'Hush!' She pulled his head down to her,
pressing her mouth against his as though there
had been enough words. Desire was rocketing
through him, made all the more powerful because
he felt the matching desire in her. His body was

so heated it was as if he was about to burst into flames. He manoeuvred his arms beneath her with the greatest care, lifting them both clear of the sofa while she clung to him, yielding so magically he moaned with the pleasure.

There were no words beyond that. Just breath-taking intensity, ecstasy to come.

Whatever the future held, they would face it together.

CHAPTER NINE

VIOLETTE DENBY drove into town, her driving fast and confident, matching her personality—or so she thought. Violette, in actual fact, drove as if no one else was on the road, or indeed had any right to be. Hairy for those coming the other way and finding Violette's car holding centre line.

Violette Danby had never been known to give ground or acknowledge that courtesy from anyone else. Violette Denby was incredibly smug. She was angry, too, and feeling betrayed. Lilli, who had followed her in all things since they were bits of kids, had gone back to Sydney with a parting shot.

'You've always been your own worst enemy, Vi! You know what I'm saying? You're a loser. I don't want to be one.'

She had been stunned by her sister's insubordination. It had struck her as bitterly cruel. Today she had a lunch appointment with the most syco-phantic of her circle, Pammy Moreton. She needed soothing, and Pammy was the one to do it. It didn't strike her as odd that she had chosen Aldo's Bistro for the lunch venue. Quite simply, it offered the best food in the town. It was a Friday, so she knew the *Outsider* wouldn't be there. She had taken over the management of Guy's restaurant while the resident chef was in Hong Kong. Violette had shut her ears to all the good things she was hearing about the new chef. Okay, the *Outsider* knew her way around a restaurant kitchen. She could cook. She could manage staff. So what if she hadn't even found her way into a kitchen yet? Cooking was not in her repertoire.

She was early for the appointment. For one thing she had a few errands to run. Things she usually got Lilli to do. The town was abuzz with people. Friday was a busy day. She acknowledged those worth saying hello to and walked determinedly past the rest.

Those stuck-up Denbys. Just about everyone hoped one day Violette Denby, the worst offender, would trip over something on the pavement and fall flat on her face.

Violette, blissfully unaware and uncaring anyway of the general disgust, was coming out of the local pharmacy when her attention was arrested by the sight of a stranger in town—a very glamorous blonde in her early thirties. Maybe she was a little bit too curvy—Violette was totally against *too* much curve—but she watched with interest as the blonde stepped away from a swish coupé, bleeping it locked over her shoulder.

Ah, one of us!

Violette licked her top lip. The big question was, who was she? What was she doing here? Most tourists spent their time in the Hunter Valley. Those whose big interest was good food and wine found their way farther on to Wangaree. Guy's restaurant had received extravagant praise from the food critics. Even she couldn't fail to notice what had been said about the current chef in the newspapers. She had brooded a whole day over that. What was so good about *tori shisomaki*—whatever that was? She'd sooner a duck mousse any day.

The blond woman—as a natural blonde herself, Violette unerringly spotted a great dye job— walked to the pavement, looking around her rather hesitantly. *Am I really going to go up to her?* Violette thought. *Yes, I am.* It wasn't the sort of thing she did with strangers, but something told her this woman was in town for a purpose. That thought stirred up memories. Hadn't Ben Mastermann, Linc's father and a prominent wool producer like her own father, remarried a few years ago? It was all coming back to her now. She was sure she had seen a photograph somewhere of the latest Mrs Mastermann—a great deal younger than her husband, and an eye-catching platinum blonde.

At the last count, two and two still made four! Now, this could be really juicy. Violette almost sprinted towards her. She might even invite Mrs Mastermann—she had a powerful perception that was who she was—to join her and Pammy for lunch. She couldn't stand Pammy's gushing *all* the time anyway. She had a little bet with herself that the glamorous Mrs Mastermann was here to pay her drop-dead sexy stepson a visit. Linc Mastermann would make any woman's sense of decency and caution twirl in the air before taking a nosedive.

Violette fixed a brilliant smile to her face. She elbowed a fellow pedestrian rudely out of the way and moved towards the other woman.

'Hello, there! You look lost.'

The woman looked back at Violette, saw a tall, equally glamorous young woman and smiled back. 'Don't I know it! I'm looking for a property called Briar's Ridge. Do you happen to know it?'

'I certainly do!'

Double whammy!

Daniela thought about leaving her mail until the following day. There was probably nothing important. It had been a long night. She'd had to break in a new assistant who was lacking confidence and she was tired. She knew it was because she was going all out to make an impression. She greatly admired Guy's resident chef, but she had her own ideas about everything. The glowing review in the papers hadn't hurt. The food writers had made big mention of her 'brilliant application of both French and Japanese cuisine'. As Carl had predicted, this stand-in time was proving her showcase.

No one was around. She parked her car on the drive and made a dash for the rows of letterboxes, key in hand. She unlocked hers quickly, then withdrew half a dozen letters and a postcard from California. That would be from an old friend who had scored a great job there.

Back in her car, she used the remote to open the huge security gates, then drove in to the basement car park. It wasn't until she was inside her apartment that she bothered to check the other mail. Two bills, one letter from Gerald—she knew his handwriting—plus another minus a postage stamp, with her name and address printed, one might have thought, by a child's hand. Wasn't that standard for an anonymous letter?

Her mind sprang to something bad. Her premonitions always had been very sharp. Should she open it? Would it matter if she tore it up? Gerald's letter bore a stamp. Then there was his fine hand-writing. Not a follow-up from Gerald, then? Not Gerald's style. It saddened her that with so much going for him Gerald Templeton was only handsome and presentable on the outside. She ran a fingernail beneath the flap. There was a photo-graph tucked inside a sheet of notepaper—very ordinary notepaper that one could buy at any supermarket. The photograph fell to the floor. She bent to pick it up, standing motionless while she studied it.

She had never seen the woman before, and she would remember her. Once seen, it was unlikely anyone would forget this women and her showgirl beauty. She was an eye-catching platinum blonde, quite shapely, expensively and very glamorously dressed. She was standing beside a car, a Mercedes. Daniela had no difficulty recognising the main street of the town.

This was no joke, and she couldn't pretend it was. The photograph had been sent with only one purpose in mind. To upset her. Daniela released a jagged sigh. The anonymity of it all was appall-ing, gutless. She hated it. People who couldn't put their name to something were always up to no good. It appeared she attracted such people.

She opened out the sheet of notepaper, stomach muscles clenching.

Don't you think your boyfriend should have told you about Stepmama? From what I hear they are way too close for comfort.

Daniela's skin tingled with shock. She was riveted by the horribleness of it all. The truly sickening thing was some part of her had been waiting for something like this. Her hand crunched up the sheet of paper in disgust before she tossed it from her. Reluctantly she took another look at the photograph, feeling as if her whole world was imploding.

She had a pretty good idea who had sent it. Violette Denby was one combative character and she emerged the clear favourite—though Daniela knew she could never prove it. The subject of the photograph just had to be Carl's stepmother.

Lover?

No way! Daniela took a deep breath, regaining her composure.

From all that had passed between them Daniela was totally convinced Carl was a moral man. What could the sender of the photograph know to back up this sick claim? It wasn't as though Carl had been deceptive about the situation. He hadn't lied. It was more he hadn't told her the truth. Was it remotely possible this woman had been involved with both father and son?

No! Her whole being screamed rejection. The

man she realised she had come to love had far too much integrity. She firmly believed that.

Or did being deeply in love with someone automatically ensure trust and a fierce loyalty?

The voice in her head required a response. What had happened to Carl to drive him away from his own home and family? He had told her since his father's latest marriage he and his brother had been virtually running the family property, one of the finest and most productive sheep stations in the country. Why would he turn his back on such family heritage and go in search of a new life? She had gathered his father had been very angry with him, seeing his moving away as a betrayal. She had tried to question him about his stepmother but he had cut her off, as though his stepmother had absolutely nothing to do with anything. She had seen the pent-up exasperation on his face at the very mention of her.

Which brought her to the question of seduction. Some women boasted with good reason of their powers to seduce. A man might find it difficult to hold out against a campaign of temptation. Could Cheryl Mastermann have constituted such a threat? And Carl had seen getting as far away from home as possible as the only way out?

Hadn't she done the same thing?

Yet here was Cheryl Mastermann, surfacing in a big way.

It didn't matter who you were, Daniela thought bleakly, or of what station in life. It was possible to be victimised. All one had to do was cross the path of one wrong person. Such people operated on an entirely different moral plane. The normal restraints most people abided by simply weren't there. The idea made her sick to her stomach.

Determined not to freak out, she ripped open Gerald's letter. If there were any more little scares in store for her, she might as well confront them. She couldn't turn away from all this. She had to get it out in the open.

It seemed there were no further threats from Gerald. Only spleen. Whatever Carl had threatened Gerald with it must have been bad, she thought wryly. A psychiatrist really should see this. It was Gerald at his very worst—or, then again, his best. Impossible as it was to believe, Gerald had convinced himself his behaviour all along had been entirely honourable. *She* was the one who should look for forgiveness. He cited a long list of her sins that went on like a criminal history. Daniela winced at the viciousness of it all. To her, it was testimony to Gerald's instability.

I hope that Aussie fool you've got yourself involved with gives you as much hell as you've given me.

For some reason that made her laugh. If Gerald didn't like the tough Australian male he should get out of this country as soon as possible.

Weekends didn't really mean a thing for the man on the land. There was always work to be done. Linc had spent the morning at the extreme end of the property, repairing a fence with Buddy. It was actually Buddy who had knocked it down when Linc had given him a go on the tractor, ploughing a fire break. Thank God *that* job was over. He and George had worked day and night getting the job done. Not that it was ever really done. Constant maintenance had to be carried out in case of cave-ins.

Spring had swung into summer, and it was getting hotter by the day—still no rain, but lots of dry storms, with spectacular cloud build-up raising hopes that were soon dashed. He had rid the property of any areas of tall grass and dried brush that could act as tinder. The homestead and all the outbuildings were well cleared. But the constant worry was that there could be someone driving through the valley who thought nothing of pitching a cigarette butt out of the window. Even in the heat the paddocks were embroidered with daisies and wildflowers and now he and Buddy rode companionably back towards the homestead, where he planned to give the shearing sheds extra attention. Buddy had the afternoon off to play cricket. From all accounts Buddy was developing into a top spinner. The Australian Cricket team was an inspiration to him, and millions of other Australian youngsters. Linc was pleased with Buddy. He was a good worker, ready to take on anything, and he was great with the horses—shoeing no problem. George Rankin had proved a fine mentor, too. Best of all, George had had a lot of experience classing superfine wool. Years before, he had topped his own wool-classing course. Linc was very comfortable in the knowledge that he and George could handle their own clip without bringing in another experienced wool-classer.

The creek, a natural fuel brake, glittered metallic in the hot sun. He parted company with Buddy and rode on. Nearing the homestead, he saw a sleek car turn into the gravelled drive. At first his mind sprang to one of the Denby sisters, but as he drew closer, familiar with luxury cars, he recognised the late-model coupé. He thought the driver was a woman. If that were the case, there was no question who it was. It had to be Cheryl, in her new toy.

He was stunned at her audacity. Unless she had his dad with her? He began to pray that was the case. Only his dad never let a woman do the driving for him, even his 'angel'! Some *angel*. He could ride away in the opposite direction, only he knew whenever he returned she would be sitting waiting for him. Cheryl didn't have angels' wings. They were more like a bird of prey's.

From her vantage point in the cool of the wide verandah, Cheryl watched for Linc to round the side of the homestead. Freshly painted, with a thick border of agapanthus lining either side of the short flight of front steps, the homestead was amazingly attractive, she thought. She could even live here. If only she had met Linc before she'd met his father! There was no justice in life. Thank God husbands could be pushed aside.

Cheryl had no idea that trying to push Ben Mastermann aside would be like trying to sidestep a charging rhino.

And here was Linc! She was hungry for the sight of him, and not ashamed to admit it. If the person who had first said 'out of sight out of mind' had met Linc Mastermann they might have changed their idea—especially if that person had been a woman. A broad-brimmed akubra covered his glossy crow-black head. It was tilted at a rakish angle. He wore a blue and white checked shirt, tight-fitting jeans, dusty boots on his feet. Inside the neck of his shirt he had wound a red bandanna, to protect his nape from the burning sun. Even his walk was so sexy she had to catch her breath.

She stood up at his approach, smoothing her tight skirt. She knew this was going to be awkward, but she thought she could handle it. She knew she looked gorgeous. One guy had once told her there were just no words to describe how gorgeous she was. Her looks, even more embellished since Linc had last seen her, always gave her a huge boost in confidence. She could coax her dear husband out of his blackest moods.

Linc spoke first. 'What the hell are you doing here, Cheryl?' he asked flatly. It was all he could do not to tell her to clear off the property and not come back. 'Where's Dad?'

At the daunting expression on her stepson's striking face Cheryl's heart began driving like a piston. His polished bronze skin was sheened with sweat. His muscular arms were grained with fine dust. God, it made her *hot*! She had never wanted a man so badly in her life.

'Is that any way to greet me?' she cooed, making her voice as sweetly innocent as she could. No mean feat, considering she was an experienced woman of the world. 'I got lonely. Your dad is in China, of all places,' she jeered.

'China is Australia's major trading partner, Cheryl,' he told her shortly, coming up the steps with that amazing easy grace. 'They're the biggest buyers of our wool and one of their most prominent new buildings is being constructed from Australian steel from the Pilbara. It might pay you to bone up.'

Cheryl dipped her platinum head. She had had her hair recoloured before she came, so she was certain of pristine roots. 'I always thought it was damaging to a woman to be too smart,' she quipped, fixing her big blue orbs on him. 'Look, I know you have every right to be angry at me, Linc,' she started quietly, just as she had rehearsed. 'My behaviour was inexcusable. I just misunderstood—'

'You certainly did.' He cut her off before she could finish her rehearsed spiel. 'Are you such a fool you could think Dad would tolerate your looking sideways at another man, let alone infidelity? You know all about his temper. He mightn't have unleashed it on you yet, but ask anyone who knows him. I'd hate to think of a bloke getting shot over you, Cheryl. You've taken a big risk even coming here. Does Chuck know?'

Again she looked at him with feigned innocence. 'No, he doesn't. I told Chuck I was spending the weekend on the Gold Coast, looking up old friends.'

'Old customers?' he asked contemptuously, pulling off the akubra and shaking his head.

Sweat had made his hair curl in tight clusters. He still wore it long on the nape. He had great hair. Something told her not to stare at him too much. Difficult when she was presented with the splendour of him. He smelt hot and spicy, but clean.

'*Girl*friends,' she corrected, pursing her full lips. She had a luscious mouth. No worries there. And she'd had all her front teeth capped. Not that there'd been anything wrong with them before, but now they were perfect. 'Could we go in? I'd love a cup of coffee.'

'Why didn't you get one in town?' he returned smartly.

'Look, Linc.' It was time to plead. 'I want us to start over.'

'Really?'

He stared her down with those shimmering silvery green eyes. She had never, ever seen eyes that exact colour. 'You must believe me. The last thing I want is to cause a rift in the family. Your father loves you. He misses you. Chuck does. So do I. We're family! We should all be friends.'

'So why didn't you tell Dad and Chuck you were going to pay me a visit?' He tossed his hat onto a planter's chair.

'A drink of cold water, then?' she pleaded, putting a perfectly manicured hand to her temple. 'The heat is making me a little sick.'

'Not pregnant, are we?' he asked satirically.

'I like to think one day I will be.' She gave him a valiant smile, though she had no intention of ever coming off the pill. She had heard that childbirth was a million times worse than root canal, never mind having a tooth capped.

'Then you better get a move on,' Linc returned harshly, having been exposed to Cheryl's little games for too long. 'Come in. I need to take a shower. I'll show you the kitchen. Maybe you can make us both a cup of coffee?'

She visibly relaxed. 'Sure!' She gave him a great big smile. She could well afford to. She knew it wouldn't be easy, but somehow she was going to get him to talk. Open up. After a while he might ease up on that spring-loaded tension which only served to make her desire him more. She was going to be a whole lot smarter this time. Jumping the gun had been her one big mistake. Usually men just rolled over when offered sex. Not Linc. She needed to get to him at a really weak moment. Maybe drunk? What she so desperately needed from him could wait a little while.

Daniela planned to be at the restaurant until around five. She liked to be early, making sure everything was in order. Saturday was their biggest night, and they had a full house. She liked to run a relaxed kitchen. Not easy, but it could be done. The team she had under her had had years of experience in top restaurants. They were highly trained, with a passion for cooking and experimentation, and they had understood immediately what she was trying to do, passionately interested in getting the formula right.

That note and the accompanying photograph had put a lot of pressure on her. She couldn't get it out of her mind. Hating what she was doing—ashamed of it, really—she rang the top hotel in the valley to ask if a Mrs Cheryl Mastermann was staying there. Surprise, surprise! They said Mrs Mastermann most certainly was, with a fair bit of gush. Unfortunately they couldn't put her through to Mrs Mastermann's suite—though she hadn't actually asked for them to do that—because the concierge had Mrs Mastermann's car ready for her. Mrs Mastermann had told them she was going out for the afternoon.

You bet she was going out for the afternoon, Daniela thought dismally. She'd have a plan. And she just bet the hotel staff had bent their heads together over *that* one. Mrs Cheryl Mastermann, and Linc Mastermann already making a name for himself in the valley. What was the connection? One thing was certain—their guest surely wasn't his *mum*.

By two o'clock Daniela knew what she was going to do. She was going to drive out to Briar's Ridge and see Carl. No reason why she shouldn't. With everything that was between them it was the normal thing to do. He wouldn't know she was coming. Ordinarily she would ring, but today she didn't.

Why, Daniela? her inner voice asked. *What's the motivation here, girl?*

It isn't a crime, is it, to be a little bit suspicious?

The trouble was, she couldn't help thinking it might be. She wanted—needed—to push her love for Carl to its outer limits. Love relied heavily on trust, didn't it? Otherwise every wife in the country would be demanding her husband fill in a daily logbook to be pored over at his return. Carl had convinced her he trusted her over what had happened with Gerald. Why couldn't she do the same for him? She could readily believe his stepmother—only a handful of years older—would be attracted to him. Carl had a powerful sexual aura. They had lived together in the same house. Probably they had gone for long rides together.

It was all her fault. Just so had Adam rounded on Eve.

Get out there to Briar's Ridge! Her inner voice told her. *Stop beating yourself up.*

The closer she drew to Briar's Ridge, the worse Daniela felt. He would hate her checking up on him. She didn't blame him. On the other hand, he didn't know anything about the 'anonymous' letter sent to her by Violette Denby. Probably Violette thought anonymous letters were just quaint little customs. Something thought up by the do-gooders of this world. If his stepmother wasn't there Daniela supposed she could say she was in the area to expand her knowledge on the valley's hot air ballooning, for example—no harm done. And Carl would conclude she couldn't wait until later tonight to see him.

If Cheryl Mastermann *was* there, what was she doing to do? She was too civilised to give in to primitive urges like pulling hair. She had a certain view of herself. Was there such a thing as an innocent visit? Of course there was.

You're talking about a blond bombshell here, girl! Innocent herself, Daniela felt very guilty.

It was a brilliantly fine day. Too fine and too

hot, with a north-westerly blowing up. People in rural areas in times of drought feared the north and north-westerlies, she had been told. The deep blue sky had an odd metallic glint, the sun beating down like an anvil. Daniela drove down the cool avenue of trees, then turned into the circular drive, the gravel almost blindingly white.

Push off again. Don't stop.

A very expensive-looking car was parked in the coolest spot beneath the overhanging grevilleas so brilliant with golden and dark pink colour.

Her inner voice suddenly chipped in. *Fight for your man. Don't you think you should?*

Daniela switched off the ignition and lifted her knuckles to her mouth. Restraint was what she did best. For all her Italian heritage, she was no simmering volcano.

This man is worth everything you've got. You want him, don't you?

She wanted *him* all right. Him and his children. Mere seconds later Daniela had transported herself to the verandah, knocking on the open door. 'Carl?'

There was a long silence. Where were they? She didn't feel up to barging in. She couldn't believe Carl might be double-crossing her, but if she found them together she might well throw up. She called out again, louder this time. Was there any such thing as lasting love, lasting fidelity?

Of course there is, girl! Think of your parents, your grandparents.

True, they had been blessed in that way. But they had been essentially good people, who'd held family very close. Carl had been brought up in a highly dysfunctional family. Sometimes people in that situation turned out very differently. His dad didn't sound like much of a role model.

What the hell? She might as well go and get it over. She was ready to *marry* him. She had even been thinking about her wedding gown. It would be glorious. She had just the style in mind. And she had begun thinking about bridesmaids. Alana, who had been so warm and welcoming, would be matron of honour, and then her first cousin Sarina, and Lyndsey, her long-time friend from their school-days and lovely Sondra in California if she could make it. If she were honest, she would have to admit she was well into the whole wedding thing, like a woman who had finally found her way.

Just as she was moving purposefully into the living room a blond woman suddenly appeared from the rear of the house. On sighting Daniela she frowned in apparent shock, and with more than a touch of indignation. 'Can I help you?' she asked sharply, regarding Daniela from head to toe.

Indeed, to Daniela's eyes it looked very much as if she was shortly to be asked to provide ID.

I'm sorry if I startled you,' she said pleasantly. You didn't hear my knock?' Best to answer question with question. 'I called out a couple of times. I'm Daniela Adami. I'm a friend of Carl's. Would he be at home?'

The woman replied with great reluctance. 'He's not right now,' she said, with an upward toss of her platinum head. She was dressed in a beautiful pink chiffon shirt with a ruby sequin trim, and a figure-hugging skirt with tiny ruby-coloured spots. Not normal dress for the country, but then she was the sort of woman who could cause city traffic jams, Daniela thought. Glitzy as they come.

'So where is he?' Daniela asked, still keeping her tone non-confrontational. Wasn't the best way to get through life to be civil? *Oh, quit being so damned polite, Daniela*, the voice in her head broke in disgustedly. 'And *you* are?' she responded to that voice, her tone picking up a brisk notch.

'I'm Cheryl Mastermann,' the woman replied, as though it was none of Daniela's damned business.

'Ah, yes.' Daniela nodded gently. 'You're Carl's stepmother. I do hope you're going to tell me his father is here? I'm so looking forward to meeting him.'

'My husband is in China,' Cheryl clipped off, not at all happy with this turn of events. The last thing she had expected was another blonde to blow her out of the water. Not that Cheryl was a blonde actually. But it hadn't been until she'd turned blonde that her love life had really taken off. The fact that Linc's visitor was a true blonde as opposed to bleached blonde, with contrasting large velvet dark eyes, only compounded her chagrin.

'So is that why you waited to visit Carl?' Daniela asked.

It was a totally unexpected broadside. This woman didn't look remotely as if she got into broadsides. 'What?' Cheryl placed her hands belligerently on her curvy hips. 'What's that supposed to mean?'

'I suppose it means exactly what you think it means, Mrs Mastermann,' Daniela said. 'Where is Carl?'

'Don't you mean Linc? Everyone calls him Linc.' Cheryl eyed Daniela with a mixture of outrage and perplexity.

'Yes, I understand that,' Daniela said. 'It's just that Carl came more naturally to me.'

'You're saying you *have* to be different?' Cheryl glared.

'No. I'm saying I have to be myself. Are you staying or are you going straight back into town, Mrs Mastermann?'

Cheryl looked taken aback. In fact she was genuinely perplexed. 'That's up to Linc,' she said. 'I've only just arrived.'

'You were planning to stay the night?'

'Look, my dear, why don't you shut the hell up?' Cheryl suddenly snapped. 'What Linc and I do is our business. This has gone far enough. I have to tell you Linc has never mentioned *you*.'

'I know someone who has!' was Daniela's instant retort. 'Violette Denby. She must have spotted you in town.'

'We had lunch, as a matter of fact,' Cheryl freely admitted. 'I liked her. She's very clued up on what's happening in the district.'

'And you told her the reason you were in the valley?'

'Of course. Listen, this is getting ridiculous. I don't have to answer to *you*.' That Cheryl was fast losing confidence, despite herself.

'You've made a mistake there, Mrs Mastermann,' Daniela told her quietly. 'Carl and I are on the point of getting engaged. Matrimony not too far behind. Neither of us can wait.'

Cheryl was poleaxed. Linc getting *married*? Hell, he hadn't even had time to settle in, let alone find a bride. Cheryl dropped all pretence of a feminine pose, even her carefully cultivated accent. 'What are you saying?' she yelled, her clear skin blotching fiercely. 'I don't believe it!'

'True.' Daniela confirmed, inclining her head. 'Surely you didn't cast yourself as in with a chance? I understand your husband is a very aggressive man. Wouldn't you find it a tad difficult trying to get away from him, even if Carl had been thinking along your lines? Death by shooting your husband might find too tame.'

Cheryl abruptly bent over, as if pain was jack-knifing through her body. Here she was thinking divorce, when Linc was thinking marriage. It couldn't be true.

Daniela made a quick move towards her. 'Mrs Mastermann, are you all right?' she asked in automatic concern.

Cheryl snapped bolt upright, eyes afire. 'You're sleeping together?' she gritted through perfect white teeth.

'Does that shock you?' Daniela spoke almost kindly.

'You realise he was sleeping with me?'

Here it is, girl. Your trust in the man you love is on the line.

'Then you'll know all about the unusual birthmark on his left flank?' Daniela said.

Cheryl hooted, surveying Daniela with scorn. 'Of course I do. For your information, I didn't mean to fall in love with Linc. I dedicated myself to acting with the utmost propriety. You've no idea how difficult it has been, trying o cauterise my emotions. It *tortured* me, living n the same house.'

'So Linc made the first move?' Daniela pressed ier for an answer.

Cheryl's hard blue eyes suddenly swam with ears. 'Do you think he didn't fight it?'

'It must have been a very grim situation,' Daniela said, implying sympathy. 'So what prought it to a head? What happened to drive him iway to seek a new life?'

'What do you *think*?' Cheryl cried with magnificent abandon. 'He was trying to do the honourable thing. So was I.'

'But you still want him?'

'And he stills wants me.' Cheryl pressed the pack of her hand against her hot cheek. Her colour had come up so fast it looked near life-threatening. 'If you're telling the truth about an engagement, it will never work. Linc is trying to forget me, but I'm in his blood.'

'Why don't we sort that out right now?' Daniela suggested. 'Just tell me where he went. If he truly loves you, it stands to reason I can't marry him.'

'Well put! I can readily understand that,' Cheryl said, at once part of the sisterhood. 'Why demean yourself by asking him, though? Why don't you simply break up with him?'

'I would like to give a reason,' Daniela said
'Where did he go?'

Cheryl became agitated. 'I have no idea!' Her
face beneath the immaculate make-up turned
abruptly from scarlet to pale as paper. 'Some rough
head, a leathery yokel called George, came to the
door. They talked a while, then Linc took off.'

'Don't worry. I'll find him,' Daniela said.

Walking back to the homestead with one eye on
the sky—it looked as though another dry storm
was not too far off—Linc thought how fortunate
he was having George. It was George's day to
visit his sister in town, but he had opted to stay
put. Like Linc and the rest of the valley, the north
westerlies had made George uneasy.

Rounding the side of the house, he saw to his
surprise Daniela's little runabout parked a few
feet from Cheryl's car. An uncontrollable anger
flared through him. Cheryl was the sort of woman
who believed she could have any man she wanted
if only she schemed hard enough. She had landed
his dad, and his dad wouldn't have been a push
over. He didn't have the slightest doubt that on
meeting Daniela Cheryl would be hell-bent on
convincing her the two of them had shared an
illicit relationship. It might be a fantasy played out
in Cheryl's head, but did Cheryl care about that'

Amazing things happened to people who thought positive. He had been hoping Cheryl would be gone by the time he arrived back. He had certainly told her that was the way to go. But Cheryl, the inveterate schemer, had held on. He hadn't been expecting Daniela until late that night, when she had finished at the restaurant. Ordinarily he would have been thrilled she had called in to see him—only Cheryl was a dangerous as a hammerhead shark.

Linc picked up pace, near running up the front steps just as Daniela was coming out of the house. 'Hi! This is a surprise.' His eyes embraced her, even as they sought to detect her mood.

'I was just coming to find you.' She sounded just the faintest bit shaken out of her natural calm. 'I've met Cheryl.'

Linc held up a darkly tanned callused hand. 'Then I have only one thing to say. It's all lies. Cheryl is having a mid-life crisis.'

Overhearing such a charge, Cheryl stalked onto the verandah, striking a familiar pose, hands on hips. 'What the hell are you talking about, Linc? Mid-life crisis? I'm only thirty-two.'

Linc slammed a hand down on the railing. 'Some people's birthdays go up. Others go down.' He turned his face to Daniela, his whole body thrumming with tension. 'She told you we were having an affair, right?'

Daniela could see the look in his glittering eyes. 'It's all right, Carl, settle down. We just had a quiet talk. Cheryl was about to leave. Weren' you, Cheryl?' She offered the woman a way out at least with some dignity.

Cheryl decided not to take it. 'Why shouldn' she know about us?' she cried angrily. 'She tells me the two of you are getting married. Don't you think you should level with her, Linc? If you don' you're running the risk she will find out about u from someone else.'

Linc made a sudden move, looking so tall and daunting both women jumped back. Cheryl into the entrance hall, Daniela barring Linc's way 'Don't—don't.' Daniela shook her head vehe mently. 'Just let her go.'

'I'd prefer to *throw* her out,' Linc gritted. 'God however was my dad fool enough to marry *you* Cheryl? If I told him about you, your marriage would be over.'

'Only you daren't tell him,' Cheryl cried breathing hard. She had reached the stage where she thought if she couldn't have Linc she'd be damned if another woman could.

Daniela acted fast. She seized the towering, mag nificently fit Linc by his two arms, applying maximum force. It was pitiful under the circumstances—he was unbelievably strong—but a symbolic gesture. 'Get your bag and go, Cheryl,' she threw over her shoulder. 'And you'd better hurry!'

'*Go!*' Linc bellowed, so loudly Cheryl yelped.

Moments later Cheryl took off, optimising all her powerful car's horse power, tyres momentarily loose in the gravel, spraying it everywhere.

'So what was the long talk about?' Linc asked, his eyes searching, grave. Cheryl's car had long since disappeared into the tunnel of trees.

'As though I can remember so far back.' Daniela tried for lightness even though she heard the hard edge in his voice. She knew he hated being forced to declare his innocence. She recognised and understood his upset.

'I know you're trying to make light of it, Daniela,' he said. 'But I *know* Cheryl. You'd better tell me.'

Daniela shook her head, trying to control her own agitation. 'I'd rather forget it. She won't be bothering you any more.'

He bit back a harsh laugh. 'Cheryl isn't famous for her IQ. And there's another worrying thing. She doesn't know my dad. I wouldn't want to be the one to try to make a fool of *him*.'

Daniela looked into his eyes, a quality of pleading in hers. 'I thought I'd put a stop to it by telling her we were getting married.' Her voice broke a little.

His heart leapt. He wanted to take hold of her and kiss her in a way that would make her completely his. Of *course* they were getting married. The sooner the better so far as he was concerned. This afternoon, if she liked.

He wasn't at all sure why he didn't cry that aloud. Instead, he asked with black humour, 'And how did she take that?' He bitterly resented Cheryl's pouring lies into Daniela's ears.

'She bent double.' Daniela opted for the truth. 'The poor woman is mad about you.'

Linc burned with the heat of impotent rage. 'She's not so much mad about *me*,' he said tersely. 'Cheryl is just plain mad. Chuck and I knew the moment we set eyes on her she was nothing but a gold-digger. If only you had known our beautiful mother!'

'If only I had,' Daniela said very gently. 'But Cheryl *is* stunning in her way.' She knew the instant she said it, it was all wrong.

Carl's eyes fairly blazed. 'Well, *I* didn't lust after her, if that's what you're implying.'

'No, no. I wasn't implying that at all.' Daniela felt her own powerful wash of anger. This was so unfair. There was a lot Carl must have to say, but he wasn't saying any of it. Was this going to develop into a fight? And all over an unscrupulous woman. So much for Carl's secret birthmark—the mark Cheryl claimed she had seen. Carl didn't have a mark on him.

Anger only seemed to ratchet up Linc's desire. This was the most captivating woman in the world. He loved the look of tenderness that was so much part of her beauty, the sheer mystery of her. He reached for her, pulling her into his arms. He could see he had made her angry, and that cut into him.

'I hate these people who try to come between us. *You're* the one I want,' he muttered with great urgency. 'I want to be inside your body. Inside your head. Behind your beautiful eyes.'

He could feel the powerful drive to make love to her. He lowered his head, taking her mouth, kissing her harder and harder, desperately wanting to wipe all memory of devious Cheryl and what she had said away. He kissed her mouth, her eyes, her neck, all over her face. Her mouth always tasted like the most delicious piece of fruit. His hands moved over her, but somewhere along the way she stopped him, her head jerking back.

'Carl!' She couldn't contain this emotional level. Though it filled her with excitement, other emotions were caving in on her.

Instantly he pulled back, his breath rasping in his throat. He felt lost and desperate. He half turned away in something like despair. Events of the past always had a hold on you.

'We're both upset,' Daniela said, coming quickly behind him and touching a tentative hand to his shoulder.

'Whatever she said, there wasn't a sliver of truth to it,' he bit off.

'I know that.' She knew he was hurting, and there didn't seem to be a thing she could do about it.

'But there were a few minutes when you doubted?' He swung back to stare down at her with brilliant, piercing eyes.

Daniela couldn't answer for a few seconds. She was a fool to feel so weak. 'Weren't there moments when *you* doubted me?' she quietly countered. They had been equally wronged.

He nodded an admission. 'But I soon got over it. You had some kind of a relationship with Templeton, however brief, and I accept his feelings became obsessive and caused you grief. Cheryl has caused *me* grief, and I had *nothing* to do with the woman. That's the thing. *Nothing!* It was all in her head. I despise her. But mud sticks.'

'Not in this case,' Daniela said, hoping the deep sincerity of her tone would calm him. 'I understand it was all untrue. Sometimes we have no control over what is happening in our lives, Carl

A lot of people could tell you about someone they've met who turned out to be destructive.'

Still the tension between them was strung out like a live wire.

Daniela sighed and dropped her hand. Maybe it was all the intensity that was in him that made him such a splendid lover. 'Anyway, she's gone and I must go, too. There are a lot of things I have to attend to before tonight.'

He shrugged, his handsome face shut tight. 'I'll walk you to your car.'

Somehow she didn't expect him to ask if she was coming back to him tonight. He didn't. That filled her with sadness. Linc Mastermann was a fine man, way out of the ordinary. He was also a complex, difficult man.

CHAPTER TEN

THE storm broke late afternoon, after hours of eerie silence. In the mood he was in, Linc had found the silence sinister. Now jagged flashes of lightning lit up a sky that was a dramatic study in silver-black, purple-black, with livid streaks of green. Great booms of thunder followed, causing squadrons of birds to take wing and head for shelter. Another dry electrical storm? Or maybe the valley would get some rain?

He continued to stand, hands clenched on the white timber banister, looking up at the sentinel hills. Fast-moving cumulus clouds scudded across the vast bowl of the sky. There was a telling smell of ozone in the air that gave some hope. On the downside, a dry wind—hot like the blast from a furnace—had picked up, stripping leaves from the trees lining the long drive and sending them into whirling spirals mixed up with the colourful kaleidoscope of spent blossom.

He felt very uneasy, and he couldn't break out of it. He knew most of it was a result of the way he and Daniela had parted. Sometimes he couldn't understand himself at all. Was he frightened of loving her so much? Was that it? Although he had always been popular enough with women, hadn't he always deliberately kept his distance? God knew he had learned the hardest lesson of all, and learned it young. Loving meant loss. Hadn't he suppressed his capacity for loving since his mother died?

He and Chuck had watched their mother grow worse and worse, then die. Their father, although profoundly affected, had survived by shutting it all out. Maybe he had a bit of his father in him? How could you love a woman as he loved Daniela yet shut her out? It didn't make a lot of sense. Sex was one thing; love was another. He had taken Daniela deeply into his heart, yet bizarrely he found himself acting as if it was just the opposite. But at least he was coming to recognise his feelings for what they were.

Fear is at the root of it, pal! his inner voice said. *Your problems hark back to your childhood.*

He felt like ringing Daniela, making contact, apologising, telling her how much he loved her and asking her if she would come back to him tonight. Only the knowledge she would be too busy to take private calls kept him from doing it. He fully intended making things right between them, but that wasn't the way life worked. No time was absolutely perfect. First there had been Templeton and then Cheryl. Linc's biggest mistake was letting such people get between him and the woman he loved.

She had gone off so sad-faced. His beautiful Daniela. He had messed up yet again. From now on in he had to focus on getting things right. To lose Daniela would break his heart.

The rain came down briefly thirty minutes later—no more than a shower bath and then the tap turned off. He was witness to a spectacular fork of lightning spearing into the hillside. Clearly it had hit a tree. Moments later he saw the upward spiral of grey smoke, an orange tint at its highest point, tapering to a dense dark grey.

There wasn't a moment to lose. He knew fires could run through open hillsides for hours before being brought under control. He had long since committed the phone number of the rural fire unit to memory, and the sooner they got here the quicker they could stop the spread of flames. He knew there was a helicopter in service. The community had raised the money to buy it with a big donation from Guy. The helicopter could drop a big payload of water and pink-coloured fire retardant on that hill. Fire travelled faster and burnt more intensely uphill than downhill.

The homestead, standing on a gentle slope within a well cleared area, was as ready as ever he and George could make it. He looked out of the open French doors in time to see George just as much on the alert as he, huffing and puffing up the front steps. Linc made the call. Smoke had turned to flame.

The minute Russ, his twenty-two-year-old assistant, raced into the Winery kitchen Daniela could tell something was wrong.

'There've been lightning strikes all over the valley,' he told them, tugging frantically at the quiff of his sandy hair. 'Those poor firies must be having a time of it. I reckon it's time for me to join up as a volunteer.' His gaze had shifted around them all. It moved from Paul, the *sous chef*, to Daniela, who had visibly paled. 'That friend of yours, Daniela— the new guy, Linc Mastermann—his property was the first to take a hit.'

'And?' she prompted, fear swelling up in her at a tremendous rate.

'That's all I can tell you.' He shrugged helplessly. 'I know the chopper's up. I saw it on the way in. The fire unit was pretty slick off the mark. I reckon if we hadn't had that heavy shower things could be a whole lot worse.'

'So the main valley road is open?' Daniela knew Russ would have had to come to work that way.

Russ slid onto a high stool, dangling his long legs. 'No problems there. The hits were on the open hillsides.'

Paul, an intensely sympathetic man, saw Daniela's distress. He and Daniela had formed a quick bond. She had met his wife, Robyn, and his two teenage girls, who had taken to her just as much as he had. Daniela was a lovely person. He regarded her not only as a colleague but a personal friend. Though Daniela didn't talk freely about her relationship with Linc Mastermann she had confided in him and Robyn that she had been seeing quite a bit of him. And Robyn, who had a sure instinct in these matters, had told him afterwards she was certain Daniela had fallen very deeply in love.

Now Daniela turned to him, the panic she was trying to hold down mirrored in her beautiful dark eyes. That tugged at him. 'Look, Paul, I know I'm asking a lot,' she said, 'but could you take over for me tonight? Everything is sorted. You're just as capable as I am.'

It wasn't strictly true, but Paul found himself nodding. 'Only one thing, Danni. You don't really know the situation. Mightn't you be putting yourself in danger?'

At that moment she didn't care. She had to get to Carl. She had to know he was safe. She had driven off with distance between them. That was terrible. She knew she didn't want to face life without him.

'Let me make a few phone calls,' Paul said, whipping out his mobile. 'If there's real trouble the restaurant won't be doing much business anyway.'

Daniela turned away to hunt up her own mobile. Carl wasn't answering. Her call went to his message bank. It struck her then how very vulnerable life was.

Small grass fires had broken out along her route, but nothing that the volunteer firefighters, ordinary valley people, couldn't cope with. Probably the grass fires had been lit by flying embers from the hills. Clouds of smoke were in the air, and the smell of burning leaves would have been wonderful had its presence not been so starkly serious. Paul had told her a house near where he and his family lived had been struck not once but twice, and had burned fiercely to the ground despite all efforts to save it. Once fire caught, it could be virtually impossible to stop.

She doubted anyone would turn up at the restaurant tonight anyway. People would stay at home to guard their properties and their precious stock.

She made the turn-off to Briar's Ridge, then drove fast down its long avenue of trees. Her very real fears began to ease. She knew just how much back-breaking work Carl and his foreman George had put in, ploughing and harrowing and clearing wide areas all around the property. She knew the creek that meandered through the property was a natural fire break.

But didn't fire skip creeks?

As she swept into the driveway she gave thanks aloud. The homestead and all the outbuildings remained untouched. It was hard to see up into the hills. Dusk had fallen and the hills were shrouded in smoke. She didn't, however, see flames. The fire unit must have arrived just in time. She parked the car right at the foot of the steps. It wasn't her imagination. The wind that drove fire had not only dropped marginally, it had dropped a lot, now blowing away from Briar's Ridge. That was a great blessing.

It was only when she stood on the verandah that she saw fire devouring a slope farther to the west. She thought that might be Narooma, the McDermott place. Her heart bled for them if it was. How did people survive the loss of everything they had worked for?

The front door was open, but Carl was nowhere around. She knew once his own property was safe he would have gone to help any neighbour in trouble. That was how the bush worked. Bred to the city, she had had no experience of fire herself, but she had seen terrible fires on television, agonised over the tragic loss of life. When Carl came home—and he *had* to come home—she would be here waiting for him. She would wait for him as long as she had to.

For ever.

It was almost midnight before he got back, driving the tractor right up to the front steps.

Danaiela flew down them, keening little cries of relief issuing from her throat. Another minute and she'd let the tears out. 'Oh, thank God, Carl! Thank God! I was so worried. Are you all right?'

Her need was so great she reached for him, not keeping in her love for him, but pouring it out.

'Easy, my love,' he breathed, as she threw herself against him. 'I'm covered in grime. You'll get it all over you.'

'As if I care!' He was indeed a mess, but Daniela was nearly dancing in an ecstasy of relief. 'Oh, Carl!' She couldn't help herself. She burst into tears, her arms coming up to lock around his neck. 'Are you hurt anywhere?' she asked, thought there was nothing she could see. He was covered in dust and grime, and darn near black, but could there be burns beneath? 'You must be sick from all the smoke you've inhaled?'

'I'm fine.' He was now, but there were some odd throbs in his exhausted body. He could handle it. He drew her back against him, vowing to never let her go. Life was a journey—not all of it good—and he had found his safe haven. When he had seen his Daniela running out of the house towards him it had fulfilled a cherished dream of coming home.

Home was this woman.

'The Gregsons have lost everything,' he told her sadly. 'Their house went up before a fire unit could get to them. The McDermotts were lucky. They've lost a lot of fencing, but no stock. We brought it all down into holding yards. Sheep will have to be put down in the Wilcox area, but the losses were minimal—considering. All property owners have been right on the ball. None of us can adequately express our gratitude to the firefighters. They're a marvellous team—so damned brave. We have to do something to raise more money for them. But right now I have to take a long shower to wash all this grime off me. Thank you for coming, Daniela,' he said, his heart bursting with love for her.

'Shh!' She placed a gentle finger against his parched lips. 'There's nowhere else I would want to be.' Her tone was exquisitely tender, like some miraculous balm.

His underlying fear of love and loss suddenly ceased to exist. Her words were like the most beautiful music he had ever heard.

Love reigned.

Arms entwined, they moved into the house. 'You're going to stay?'

She allowed herself her first laugh of the night. 'I haven't got my nightie.'

His arm tightened around her narrow waist. His woman. His soon-to-be wife. 'You won't be needing it,' he said.

For those fortunate enough to find a soul mate in life, dreams really did come true.

EPILOGUE

IN ACCORDANCE with tradition, the engagement party for Daniela and Linc would be hosted by Daniela's parents, Marc and Lucia. Linc had formally asked Marc for his daughter's hand in marriage as a mark of respect, and it was one Daniela's parents found both charming and affecting. In fact, in the weeks preceding the engagement party, Linc endeared himself to the entire Adami family. As far as they were concerned their Daniela had got things just right. This was a fine young man—one they were full of enthusiasm to make an important member of their family.

It was an excited Lucia who came up with the idea of a theme for the engagement party, only she was a little tentative about how they would take it. She had thought herself it would be glorious fun, and would give the young women in particular a great opportunity to dress up.

Twenty young couples had been decided upon,

and the party would take the form of a banquet, catered by the family and celebrated at their new restaurant. They had become so popular, especially since Daniela had returned home, that they had desperately needed bigger and better premises. They had retained the name Aldo's, but the new restaurant was almost three times as big, and much better situated, with a lovely view of the town park. Its décor showed the family's Italian background. They had even imported from Italy six beautiful hanging light fittings like great starbursts. They had set them back quite a bit, but had proved well worth the money. These light fittings had been the inspiration for Lucia's plan.

'I thought Renaissance?' She launched into this plan one Sunday night, over a family dinner, examining each face in turn. 'Beautiful long floating dresses for the young women, lots of sparkle, gem-encrusted bodices, costume jewellery, perhaps an elaborate hairdo. Some licence for the young men, who mightn't fancy the idea of wearing tights and tunics?' A quick sideways glance at Linc. 'Maybe a very fancy flounced shirt, fitted black trousers? Perhaps a velvet cap?'

Silence around the table. Aldo rolled his bottom lip over his top one, considering.

'Of course it's only an idea,' she said hurriedly. 'I thought a theme would be nice. Maybe the great lovers of history, literature, grand opera?' she suggested. 'I so want this great occasion to be truly memorable for you both.'

'It's brilliant!' Linc suddenly declared, with Daniela not far behind. How could he pass up the opportunity of seeing his Daniela as a ravishing Renaissance promised bride? He didn't know if he could manage the tights but, hell, there was nothing wrong with his legs—and Lucia *had* given the guys an out.

As it turned out, the engagement party was a night to be remembered by everyone who attended. The young men had entered fully into the spirit of the occasion, hiring costumes that, even if they weren't absolutely Renaissance, certainly allowed them to cut dashing figures. In fact they looked amazing! This added greatly to the general excitement. And the twenty young women—a group that included Alana Radcliffe, who had finally returned from her honeymoon—looked ravishing. Lyrical figures from the past. All of them had taken great care, searching for just such a costume that would make them appear at their most magical. The results were truly wonderful, and the gala evening was given an extra charge.

It was an engagement party to dream of. The food was superb, and the wine, the music. The room had the fragrance of roses. Roses for love. The marvellous glass light fittings above the tables lent young faces and flesh a most tender bloom.

Daniela, wearing a seriously beautiful and extravagant long dress in gold silk with a train, moved a hand over her beautiful engagement ring, letting it still over the dome of the central diamond, a large flawless stone flanked by more diamonds of a carat and more. She thought it the most beautiful ring she had ever seen.

Linc, who was getting enormous pleasure out of seeing her constantly doing this, bent his face to her, a smile in his brilliantly glimmering eyes. 'I'm thrilled you love your ring, my love. Other precious stones are lovely, but to me the diamond is the jewel of jewels! As you are mine.'

Very gently, exquisitely, their lips met. 'It's perfect,' she murmured, gazing lovingly into his eyes.

'And I've never seen you looking more beautiful,' Linc spoke again, piercingly aware he had never felt happier in his life.

'All for you,' Daniela whispered back. 'Mamma's idea was a *coup*. Everyone looks so marvellous. Ordinary evening dress couldn't have made such a spectacle. I almost feel like I'm back in the Renaissance. I'm so proud of what my family have done for us tonight.'

'My family, too, now,' Linc said, happy it was true. 'You look ravishing.'

At the naked look of love and desire in his eyes she let her blond head, piled into an elaborate coiffure set with jewels, fall gently onto his shoulder. Tonight he wore an ornate velvet jacket, sleeveless, ruby-coloured, heavily embroidered in gold, over a splendid white flounced shirt with black moleskins. Not for one moment had he appeared uncomfortable in such flamboyant garb. He looked stunning.

Beautiful—all beautiful! Daniela thought. She couldn't wait until she and her father were walking up the aisle, with her beloved Carl waiting for her at the altar. His brother Charles, who was to be their best man, was here tonight with his sweet-faced companion, a lovely young woman called Louise. And a wedding invitation had been sent to Carl's father which naturally had had to include Cheryl. They had readily accepted. No doubt Cheryl had convinced herself her trip to Briar's Ridge had been a harmless piece of fun, Daniela thought. But none of that mattered any more. They had invited Rose Denby and her Simon to the party, but Rose's two older sisters had made things easy by removing themselves to Sydney. Daniela was on Cloud Nine with happiness, and wished everyone in the world well.

'Love…' Linc's wine-scented breath caressed her cheek. 'It's the doorway to heaven,' he pronounced.

He was right, of course.

MILLS & BOON
Romance

On sale 7th November 2008

*Get into the Christmas spirit this month as
Mills & Boon® Romance brings you…*

WEDDED IN A WHIRLWIND *by Liz Fielding*

Miranda is on a dream tropical island holiday when disaster
strikes! She's stranded in a dark cave…and she's not alone.
Miranda is trapped with macho adventurer Nick – and the
real adventure is just about to begin…

BLIND DATE WITH THE BOSS *by Barbara Hannay*

Sally has come to Sydney for a fresh start. And she's trying
to ignore her attraction to her brooding boss, Logan.
Fun-loving Sally has waltzed into Logan's life and it will
never be the same again…

THE TYCOON'S CHRISTMAS PROPOSAL
by Jackie Braun

With the dreaded holidays approaching, the last thing widowed
businessman Dawson needs is a personal shopper who wants to
get *personal*. Eve is determined that the festive fun begins!

CHRISTMAS WISHES, MISTLETOE KISSES
by Fiona Harper

Louise is determined to make this Christmas perfect for her and
her young son. But it's not until she meets gorgeous architect
Ben that her Christmas really begins to sparkle…

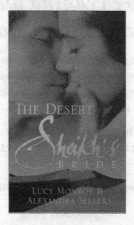

Celebrate 100 years of pure reading pleasure with Mills & Boon®

To mark our centenary, each month we're publishing a special 100th Birthday Edition. These celebratory editions are packed with extra features and include a FREE bonus story.

Plus, you have the chance to enter a fabulous monthly prize draw. See 100th Birthday Edition books for details.

Now that's worth celebrating!

September 2008

Crazy about her Spanish Boss by Rebecca Winters
Includes FREE bonus story
Rafael's Convenient Proposal

November 2008

**The Rancher's Christmas Baby
by Cathy Gillen Thacker**
Includes FREE bonus story *Baby's First Christmas*

December 2008

One Magical Christmas by Carol Marinelli
Includes FREE bonus story *Emergency at Bayside*

Look for Mills & Boon® 100th Birthday Editions at your favourite bookseller or visit
www.millsandboon.co.uk

4 FREE

BOOKS AND A SURPRISE GIFT!

We would like to take this opportunity to thank you for reading this Mills & Boon® book by offering you the chance to take FOUR more specially selected titles from the Romance series absolutely FREE! We're also making this offer to introduce you to the benefits of the Mills & Boon® Book Club—

- ★ **FREE home delivery**
- ★ **FREE gifts and competitions**
- ★ **FREE monthly Newsletter**
- ★ **Exclusive Mills & Boon® Book Club offers**
- ★ **Books available before they're in the shops**

Accepting these FREE books and gift places you under no obligation to buy, you may cancel at any time, even after receiving your free shipment. Simply complete your details below and return the entire page to the address below. You don't even need a stamp!

YES! Please send me 4 free Romance books and a surprise gift. I understand that unless you hear from me, I will receive 6 superb new titles every month for just £2.99 each, postage and packing free. I am under no obligation to purchase any books and may cancel my subscription at any time. The free books and gift will be mine to keep in any case.

N8ZED

Ms/Mrs/Miss/Mr .... Initials ....
BLOCK CAPITALS PLEASE

Surname ....

Address ....

....

.... Postcode.............................

Send this whole page to:
UK: FREEPOST CN81, Croydon, CR9 3WZ

Offer valid in UK only and is not available to current Mills & Boon® Book Club subscribers to this series. Overseas and Eire please write for details and readers in Southern Africa write to Box 3010, Pinegowie, 2123 RSA. We reserve the right to refuse an application and applicants must be aged 18 years or over. Only one application per household. Terms and prices subject to change without notice. Offer expires 31st December 2008. As a result of this application, you may receive offers from Harlequin Mills & Boon and other carefully selected companies. If you would prefer not to share in this opportunity please write to The Data Manager, PO Box 676, Richmond, TW9 1WU.

Mills & Boon® is a registered trademark owned by Harlequin Mills & Boon Limited. The Mills & Boon® Book Club is being used as a trademark.